Stealing Liberties
Task Force 125, Book #4

Lisa Pietsch

Table of Contents

Copyright   1

Task Force 125 Series   2

Prologue   3

One   4

Two   14

Three   23

Four   30

Five   37

Six   49

Seven   59

Eight   69

Nine   78

Ten   93

Eleven   108

Twelve   118

Thirteen   126

Fourteen   133

Fifteen   147

Sixteen   157

Enjoy A Sneak Peek Of Freedom's Price, Book 5 in the Task Force 125 Series   162

    Chapter 1   162

About The Author   168

Copyright

Published by Defiance Press & Publishing, LLC

Bulk orders of this book may be obtained by contacting Defiance Press & Publishing, LLC. www.defiancepress.com.

Defiance Press & Publishing, LLC

281-581-9300

info@defiancepress.com

Task Force 125 Series

The Path to Freedom
A Taste of Liberty
Freedom's Promise
Stealing Liberties
Freedom's Price

Prologue

Moscow

Konstantin folded the dead man's lifeless limbs around the still warm torso and tucked the corpse into the large plastic garment bag before zipping the makeshift body-bag closed. He hefted the awkward package over his shoulder and dropped it into the trunk of his BMW with a *thunk*. He slammed the trunk closed and walked around the sedan to climb into the driver's seat.

His phone chirped.

Konstantin pressed the button on the steering wheel to answer as he started the car. "Da."

"I have a cleaning job for you."

Konstantin recognized Nikolai Federov's voice. "Good. I just finished the last one." Nikolai's childish grudges over social slights had been keeping Konstantin busy with hits for the past several weeks, but who was Konstantin to judge? Nikolai's ultra-sensitive, paranoid personality, mixed with his deep pockets were about to finance Konstantin's early retirement.

"This one has three parts, all foreign, all highly skilled, and there's a bonus."

Konstantin considered the possibilities. Foreign hits were more difficult because they involved acquiring weapons after traveling into a foreign country. Travel itself posed a challenge as he was barred from several countries already. A highly skilled target was one he couldn't pass up though. Most of his hits had been ducks in a barrel. Boredom had set in lately and a challenge could bring back the spark. A target with skills would be a pleasure. He grinned as he drove off the gravel road and onto the highway. "Ahh…I love a good challenge."

"Come to my office for the details."

"I'll be there."

One

Vince Hennessee lay in bed, unable to sleep, staring at the ceiling and listening to Sarah's soft breathing. She'd gone to sleep soon after they'd made love. She'd probably sleep for quite some time. Sarah Stevens was the kind of woman he'd always wanted. She was strong and capable one minute, and soft and loving the next. She was a mix of exquisite contradictions. She had the world by the balls and she was beginning to know it. Any man would be a fool to let her slip away, and Antonia Hennessee didn't raise any fools. The only problem was timing. He'd done something against his better judgment after Sarah and the team rescued him from Nikolai's compound. He'd spent a magical week alone with Sarah on the island he'd bought with gun money, courtesy of, but unbeknownst to the U.S. government. The lure of an idyllic life together had been too much. He'd presented her with a four-carat diamond and asked her to marry him even though he knew their timing was all wrong and they'd have to set aside their love affair to get back to the work of being Paramilitary Operations Officers with the Central Intelligence Agency. He gave a short chuckle at the title. They were spies who specialized in wet-work, assassinations, for "the agency". Relationships didn't always pan out for clandestine agents working undercover, and life as a Force Recon Marine had never been conducive to a happy home life, but Vince reveled in the dream of domestic bliss with the right woman. Being here with someone like Sarah was what he wanted, all he'd ever wanted.

He rested his arm on his forehead. *Is it too much to ask for just a simple, uncomplicated life?*

Nikolai Federov, the Russian mob captain they'd failed to liquidate during their last mission who had subsequently succeeded in kidnapping Vince, was still at large, and that meant Federov still had guys watching Sarah. She and Vince might have everything they needed, but a simple, happy life would always be tenuous at best until they found Nikolai and buried him. Thanks to a very generous, and now deceased, ex lover, Sarah had all the money she'd ever need to assume an alias, so she'd just given the CIA their walking papers and told the Agency she was leaving the business. Guilt tore at Vince. Nikolai's life had to end if theirs was to begin, and it wasn't right to let Sarah believe they had a chance at making a future together yet.

Maybe we can get Nikolai quickly and then run away together?

The cell phone on the bedside table rang and interrupted his dark thoughts. He snatched it up and quickly checked the time. The screen said five AM. He rolled his eyes and tried to keep his voice low. "Hennessee."

Sarah reached over, her eyes still closed, and laid a soft, warm hand on his shoulder.

Vince turned his head toward the touch and gently kissed a newly manicured fingertip.

"It's Philippo. If anyone asks, I didn't tell you but there's a contract out on you."

Vince's stomach tumbled. He'd played spy games with the world's worst bad guys for years but this was the first contract put out on him. If Philippo felt it was worth calling about then the reward offered had to be a big one. Vince gently moved Sarah's hand onto his pillow and slid off the bed. He held the phone between his chin and shoulder as he slipped on a pair of Jeans. He'd been expecting this after Federov escaped when the team rescued him and destroyed Federov's compound in Saudi Arabia. What he really needed to know was how big the price tag was so he'd know what kind of contract killers to expect. "How much?" He plodded barefoot into Sarah's kitchen to make some coffee.

"Three hundred thousand dollars each for you, Will Adams, and Sarah Stevens. An extra hundred thousand bonus has been offered for anyone who can take down all three of you."

This is serious shit.

Vince grunted. "Not a bad price."

Not a good situation. A Russian'll do a street hit anywhere in the country for a grand. This kind of money would bring out the big players, the Ukrainian hit men that would track their targets around the world like dogs, stuff them in a box and ship them first class to the client who posted the contract.

He pushed the button to start the already prepared coffee maker.

Gotta love that girl's nightly routine.

5

"A million for the whole set, huh?"

"I'm afraid so, my friend."

Vince bit his lip and considered which hit men he knew who would likely take the challenge. A few good ones came to mind. "Any takers on the contract yet?"

The coffee maker gurgled and his stomach growled.

"A few up-and-comers, mostly Ukrainians. You know how they love big game."

"Thanks, Phil."

"Good luck."

Vince clicked off and set his cell phone on the kitchen counter.

This kind of contract could make a man's career a legend.

He poured two cups of coffee and his phone rang again.

"Vince. It's Mark Davidson."

"Hey, Mark. How are you?" Vince drank from his cup, grateful for the warm liquid that would power him through what was shaping up to be a hard day.

"I'm doing well, thanks. Listen, this isn't really a social call. I wanted to let you know I've received an assignment transfer."

"Oh, yeah? Where to?"

"Buffy and I thought it would be nice to see Moscow. She's crazy for shopping and the furs are ridiculous."

Vince smiled. "Buffy's a spitfire, but give me a happy housewife any day. You're a good man to plan around your wife's shopping needs."

"Yeah, so she tells me."

"Are you there now?" Vince rubbed the back of his neck. Davidson was a power player in the CIA. This phone call had to be important.

" We just moved in and I've had a few days at the office. You'll never guess who I heard was in town."

"Hmm…" Vince took another drink of coffee and set his cup back on the counter. "An old, not so friendly friend of mine named Nikolai, maybe?"

"That's right. Seems he's come back to the bosom of the motherland to feel the love, so to speak."

"That's good to know, Mark." Vince rubbed his eyes with his free hand. A dull ache throbbed in the center of his forehead.

"I don't know what your plans are, but if you decide to come out for a visit, I could make some arrangements for you, put you in touch with some people who might help you out."

"As a matter of fact, I was just getting my travel plans together for a little trip out that way."

"Excellent. Let me talk to a friend of mine and I'll email you some information later today. Do you have a flight yet?"

"I'll leave tomorrow."

Sarah won't be happy, but she understands the nature of the spy business and will eventually understand. The sooner we get this done, the sooner we can get married, have a half dozen kids and a happy life in Idaho.

"Good. Word has it Nikolai is working on some projects that may be of interest to both of us. The sooner you pay a visit the better."

You mean the sooner I kill him, the better. CIA desk jockeys were all the same. They all wanted to put hits out on new targets, but while the field agents like Vince were getting blood on their hands, guys like Davidson were buying their wives minks or new boobs.

"I'll be waiting for that email. Thanks for the call, Mark."

"No problem, Vince. Stay safe."

Vince clicked off, slipped the phone into his pocket and grabbed both coffee mugs before walking back into Sarah's bedroom.

~~~

Sarah watched Vince walk into the room looking like he carried the weight of the world. An icy trickle of apprehension flowed down her spine. "What is it?"

Vince walked over to her side of the bed and smiled as Sarah sat up. He handed her a cup of coffee as he sat on the edge of the bed and took a sip of his own. "A friend of mine in the contracts business just called. Nikolai's got contracts out on us."

Sarah nodded. "We expected that." She put her coffee cup on the bedside table and tried to reassure him with a gentle hand on his shoulder. "We've got aliases and enough money to go anywhere. He'll never find us."

"We can't run. He's offered a high price." He shook his head. "I should have known we couldn't pull this off yet."

She snuggled against his shoulder and ran her hand along his thigh. Confusion hit Sarah as she saw an unsure Vince for the very first time. "We can do this together. We've got the resources and the connections we need to quit this life and start one together. Let the next agents in line take on Nikolai."

"You know we'll never be safe until we find him. It'll always be him or us." He looked down at his knees. "We can do this, but we'll be sitting ducks if we try to do it together."

"Why? We're a good team." Her gut told her he'd already made a decision and this wasn't going to be a discussion but a notification. She wasn't ready to accept what she suspected he was about to do. "Vince, we can do this!"

"Don't you see, Sarah? When Nikolai kidnapped me, the Agency wrote me off. As far as they're concerned I'm missing in action. I can go anywhere now."

"Yes, and so can I. My contract with the Agency has been cleared. They accepted my resignation." Sarah's stomach knotted. She rubbed her eyes and wondered how she could convince Vince not to do this on his own. He seemed too unsure of himself to handle it, and she wondered why she'd never seen this side of him before. "What are you trying to tell me, Vince?"

Vince stood and took a deep breath before he spoke. He turned to face her. "If you take one more assignment with the team, we'll have a chance to draw Nikolai out. He wanted us before, but he's hot for our heads now that he's seen his house leveled to rubble and dust."

He hates the idea of me working for the Agency. He's mentioned it a hundred times in the past three weeks. Why his sudden weakness and indecisiveness?

Sarah jumped up and stood toe to toe with Vince. "What the hell? No way!" Sarah turned and paced a few steps before turning back to glare at Vince. "I've already resigned my position with the agency. They've closed my file and I have a new identity."

"Don't you see?" He seemed earnest. "If you take another assignment and leave your party girl trail, he'll be all over you."

Is this some kind of fucked up loyalty test to see if I'll take the bait? He knows I loved that job but I gave it up because he wanted me to.

"Let me get this straight." She held her fist up and raised a finger to make each successive point. "I have a villa in Italy with a profitable vineyard, a condo in Las Vegas, and more money than God, but instead of just running away together to live the good life, you want me to take another assignment and go fuck some bad boy on the CIA's most wanted list?" In all the assignments she'd taken, she'd had to play the Honey Pot, the sex kitten they dropped in to bait the target. This was the first time she'd ever felt like someone was pimping her out, and it was Vince doing it. She raised her voice now but she didn't give a damn. What he was suggesting was cowardly, foolhardy and stupid when an easy out stared them in the face. "You want me to leave a trail so you can get a second shot at Nikolai when the first one went so well?"

He flinched and stared at her, wide-eyed.

The last comment was meant to hurt him. Nikolai had been a step ahead of Vince when he'd left Italy to assassinate Federov. Nikolai had Vince kidnapped instead. If Sarah and the rest of the team hadn't pooled their resources, broken a lot of international laws, and had some damned good luck, Vince would be in a shallow grave somewhere in Saudi Arabia right now. She rubbed her forehead. "Who are you? And what have you done with Vince Hennessee?"

"No, baby." Vince reached out to her but she deflected his grasp and glared at him instead. "No. I'm talking about being able to protect you. If you're the bait, I can circle around and get him before he takes his shot at you."

Fuck that. Your skills have been slipping.

Her faith in his abilities was waning fast, and this last attempt of his hadn't helped. Her stomach turned as she realized she couldn't trust him. She shrugged him off and continued pacing. "No, I don't like it. There's too much risk. I don't like it at all." She balled her fists at her side and eyed him. She hated that she couldn't trust him to have her back and make a simple hit. But she had to follow her gut. "While you're out there, who'll have your back? You'll be on your own with no support at all. What if something happens to you again?"

Because it will.

Sarah bent to pick up a T-shirt he'd left lying on the floor. "I don't want to go through that again." She threw the T-shirt into the laundry basket in the corner and continued pacing. She softened her tone, hoping to appeal to Vince's feelings for her. "Do you have any idea how hard it was for me to just stand there while Nikolai's goons tied you to a chair and beat you to a bloody pulp?" Her voice cracked and she hated herself for the weakness it showed. "Do you have any idea what that did to me?" He'd walked himself into a trap and she'd had to witness his torture firsthand. It had torn at her heart then as it did now, but fear had given way to pity.

He's lost his edge.

Vince grabbed Sarah by the shoulders and fixed her with his soft brown gaze. "And do you have any idea what it would do to me if Nikolai got *you*? He'd do much more than slap you around and break a few ribs. Sarah, they'd do the worst things a man can do to a woman. You would die a slow, painful, gruesome death."

She shuddered. She'd heard the rape and torture stories. There was a special briefing just for women who joined the clandestine service to prepare them for what could happen if they were captured.

He trailed his fingers gently down her arms to hold her hands. "You've got to understand. I've been doing this sort of thing for a long time. I know how these people think. We can make this plan work so nobody but Nikolai will get hurt."

You aren't the man I thought you were. You've let your emotions take control of that once analytical mind. Running off half-cocked to save me is not a strategy.

Sarah's heart ached. She used to think she wanted to settle down with a guy like Vince and live happily ever after, but how would she find happily ever after knowing he could be so weak and unsure of himself? Flashbacks from the past year played out at hyperspeed inside her mind. Vince had taken a taxi to a commercial airport and got kidnapped before he even made it past security. That wasn't the work of a seasoned spy. The job in Italy went to shit and they lost good men. Even Sarah had taken a bullet.

He'[d grown sloppy. After only two years in the agency, and she knew it. What was his excuse after years in the Marines and just as many years as an arms dealer for the agency? Her assumptions and the dreams of her past slipped away. No, this was not the future she wanted. She shook free of his grasp, took a deep breath and a stepped back. "No." She shook her head. "There has to be another way."

Vince grabbed Sarah around the waist and pulled her close.

She turned to look away.

"What do you think I've been doing for the past week? I lie awake at night trying to work out how we can get our happily ever after. I've worked through every scenario a hundred times in my head. The only thing that makes sense is for us to bait and flank him. It's the only way."

Sarah sighed and looked at a once great man now grasping at straws. Her voice softened and she touched his cheek. "Wake up Vince. We aren't going to get that happily ever after."

"We still can. We can still have it all, Sarah. Just not yet. One more job and we can do it."

We need to face the truth. We're targets for too many terrorists. Everybody wants us dead.

Sarah hugged Vince, holding on to him as dreams from a past life washed away like sand under the tide. This morning her life had changed completely. Or maybe it had been changing over the past two years and she was only now seeing what it had become? Her head and her gut told her that tactically, baiting Nikolai and assassinating him was the right move, but having Vince out there alone to take the shot after he'd lost his edge was wrong. He needed the whole team to make it work.

We might get Nikolai but we'll never be together.

She hadn't wanted to fall in love again. She'd had no intention of doing so. This morning, she'd realized she'd fallen out.

He must know it too.

Her heart ached.

"I've spoken to Mark Davidson. He's been transferred to Moscow and has some people keeping an eye on Nikolai."

Sarah broke from Vince's grasp and walked to the sliding glass door that led out to the patio of her luxury condo at The Signature at MGM Grand.

The sun was coming up in Las Vegas and the staff was arranging the chairs by the pool far below.

Mark is a player, not a killer. Vince needs real men behind him on this operation.

"If Mark has people on him why can't he just make Nikolai disappear? Why can't we hire a gun to do it for us?"

Vince inhaled hard through his teeth. "You know it doesn't work like that. Mark has an official cover with his state department job. If he uses that job to go out and exterminate some Russian, he's looking at prison time, quite possibly in Russia. Do you have any idea what the Russian prison system is like?"

Her cheeks burned and she blinked hard to hide the angry tears that had formed.

I never cry. I never fucking cry except when I'm mad as hell and then it just looks weak.

She lowered her voice to a growl. "How many languages do I speak? How many dead men have underestimated me, just like you're doing now? Do you mean to tell me you still think I'm just another pretty face? After two years of operations and me putting my life on the line for you more than once, you still think I'm just a frail, dumb woman?" She swallowed the ball of bile she wanted to spit at Vince and ran a hand through her hair. "Screw you. Don't let my cover confuse you as to who I really am." She spun around to shoot lightning bolts at the wall so she wouldn't punch him in the face.

His breath was slow and loud behind her. "Look, we can do this ourselves. Davidson has some connections I can use. The team has a mission brief the day after tomorrow so I'll leave for Moscow tomorrow."

And you'll die there unless you suddenly pull a guardian angel out of your ass.

Sarah turned to see him sitting on the edge of the bed, shoulders slumped. The magic they'd shared together had been sucked out of the room. She didn't know the man sitting on her bed.

They'd only had a couple weeks together. It had been like a honeymoon, the two of them on their own island, making love, swimming, lying around with no worries and nobody to bother them. It had been idyllic. Now they were back in Las Vegas and the only mirage left was the hotel on the strip.

Vince's phone rang, and she watched as he pulled it from his pocket.

"It's Davidson." He never hesitated to answer it.

Reality hit. It was over. He had no intention of ever discussing any of this with her to get her input. His plan was to throw her out there as bait. Chum for the sharks.

Well, fuck you.

She walked into the kitchen and placed a call of her own.

"Full name please?"

"Sarah Marie Stevens."

"How may I direct your call?"

"Young."

Sarah waited while the operator at The Camp connected her to the man who was her team's handler. The man who had just recently accepted her resignation. Their team, American Swift, was like every other paramilitary team in The Agency's arsenal. They had a 'handler'. Colonel Young was a monster of a man with a chest the size of Mount McKinley and biceps to match. Sarah suspected he was at least part Samoan but never bothered to ask as he was never one to encourage chit-chat. For good reason too. Colonel Young worked in that black world where the U.S. military and her spies mixed to create the most deadly personnel possible, those with intelligent, analytical minds and a patriotic streak so wide they could look at a human being, see a target and eliminate it without remorse. "Wetwork" was the impersonal, industry term for American Swift's line of work.

"Hey, Sarah, how's retired life?"

"Put me back in."

"I knew you'd be back. See you tomorrow."

What was the world coming to when a prick like Young knew her better than her fiancé did? She paused a moment as she realized spy work was her element but love scared the hell out of her.

Maybe I have more in common with the pricks than the heroes now? Maybe the pricks are the real heroes? I don't really care anymore.

Two

London

The smell of Captain Black tobacco hung in the air and mingled with the scent of burning wood from the large stone fireplace that warmed the Rose & Crown Pub. Jay Stanstead had been all over the world, but this pub, in this little London neighborhood where he grew up was always home.

"So how's retired life treating you, mate? Nothing like the excitement we had back in the services, eh?" Ian Urquhart tipped his Guinness back and took a big gulp.

Jay smiled at his old friend from the forces, who had retired with him a year ago, as Ian gushed on about a new job he'd landed as a mercenary. They'd been delivered to every hellhole and hotspot known to man, and some unknown, only to live to tell the tales, unlike too many of their brothers in arms. When they retired, Ian ran off to find more adventures as a soldier of fortune and Jay went home to London for a nice peaceful retirement.

"How'd you like to have the same sort of adventures at ten times the pay?" Ian Urquhart waggled his red eyebrows and his green eyes sparkled as he handed Jay a business card.

A half-million quid annually seemed too good to be true and Jay knew if something seemed too good to be true it usually was. Jay read the card. "Brock Benjamin. Sentrion Services." He glanced up at Ian and took a long drink of his Guinness. "What's this? Your mercenary master?" He tossed the card back at Ian.

"It's a P.M.C., you wank. Nobody says 'mercenary' anymore."

"Private military company, mercenary...it's all the same. You're a gun for hire. That's not for me, mate. I'm done fighting. I've done twenty years in Her Majesty's service, and I'm respectably retired now."

Ian leaned back in his chair and winced. "You're still a young man. Retired doesn't mean dead, Jay. Every day is the same for you. You're slowly dying and you can't even see it."

He was probably right, but Jay was tired of taking bullets with no benefits. He wanted to live a little. Granted, he hadn't done a whole lot of living lately, but it would happen. Jay leaned back in his seat. "Look at me." Jay spread his arms and grinned. "I'm far from dying. I made some very good investments over the years and I've got a nice retirement compliments of queen and country." He patted his stomach. His abs were still as ripped as they had been a year ago when he finished his last tour in Iraq. "This is the good life, mate."

"Bollocks!" Somebody slammed a glass onto a table behind Jay. "It's the worst life for a fighting man."

Jay spun around to see who had interrupted them. An old man sat in the corner of the pub by the great stone fireplace. He looked about a hundred years old. He pointed to Jay with a crooked, arthritic finger. "I used to feel the same way you do. Sergeant Nicholas James, retired, Royal Marines."

Jay nodded in deference to the man for his years of service. "What changed your mind?"

"I made that same choice thirty years ago. I thought I wanted to settle down, live the easy life. It worked out well for a few years. Met a cracking bird, even married her, but I couldn't stop looking for the action. I found it in all the wrong places. Finally she couldn't put up with it any longer and left me. I've been on my own, drinking my days away here ever since. Take the action, lad. You'll be dead like me without it."

Bloody hell! Talk about putting the fear of God into a man!

Jay raised his glass to the man. "Here's to your service. Thanks for the advice, sergeant. I'll take it into consideration."

The old man shook his head. "Don't waste time, lad. You spend all those years in foxholes, mucking about in the third world convincing yourself that the grass is greener on the other side, well I've seen the other side, mate, and it's rubbish. Bloody rubbish. Live while you're alive. Grab your bollocks and your kit and get the hell out of here. Anywhere beats sitting here waiting for something to happen because I'll tell you, in the past thirty years not one bloody thing has happened in this stinking place."

Ian raised his bushy eyebrows at Jay. "How about it?"

Jay slid the knuckles of his left hand under his chin and stroked the soft beard that had grown over the past week. "Better give me the card."

Ian smiled and slid the business card back across the table.

15

The old man hunched over his pint once more. "Well done, lad. You won't regret it."

I'm sure I will.

Las Vegas

Sarah watched as the plane Vince had boarded took off. Mark Davidson had found tickets on booked flights and Vince was packed and on a plane to Moscow within an hour of their conversation this morning. She waited until the plane was a silver speck in the sky and then reflected for a moment on the fact that not one tear fell. Maybe it had just been physical attraction? No, it was more than that. Maybe it was because he was so damned manly and a take-charge guy. She'd never met anyone like him before and that had been so refreshing. So much about herself, her life and her dreams had changed in the past two years. Though she hated giving up on anything, especially relationships with good men who were so few and far between, she knew she couldn't commit to him. She hadn't seen him clearly and she knew damned well he had no idea who she really was either.

I've got my looks, a ton of money and a risky job to keep me busy. It could be worse. I could be fat and homeless like I was two years ago.

Her phone rang. The four carat diamond Vince had given her caught on the pocket of her jeans as she pulled the phone out.

Oh, shit! I should have given that back.

She looked at the caller ID. It was Will Adams, the team's second in command, first now that Vince was gone.

"Talk to me, boss."

"Welcome back! Meet us at Brian's house as soon as you can today. There's somebody you need to meet before we see Young tomorrow."

"I'm leaving the airport now. I'll be there in ten minutes."

Sarah pocketed the phone and left the terminal. On auto pilot she lit a cigarette on her way out the door and walked through the parking garage to her Jeep. She hopped in and drove away from McCarran International Airport. The old Sarah and her old dreams of home and hearth were gone. It felt like starting over again, like she had two years ago when the Air Force kicked her out and the CIA took her in. Oddly conflicted in this 'no man's land' of her soul, the drive to Brian's was a blur. In this life, all she'd ever have was herself.

London

Jay wrapped a towel around his waist as he stepped out of the shower and picked up the ringing phone. "Hello."

"Jay Stanstead?"

"Yeah."

"Brock Benjamin."

Jay ran a hand over his short, wet hair. "Well, that was quick."

"I don't like to waste time. I'll get right to the point. You have an impressive resume and I'd like to put you to work for Sentrion right away. How soon can you come to the United States?"

"I'll have to check the airlines but I suppose I could leave right away."

"Great. I'll have my assistant take care of the travel arrangements and call you back. I'll see you tomorrow."

Jay wondered what he'd gotten himself into. The last thing he wanted to do was muck about in the mountains of Afghanistan again.

I'm not taking crap jobs for kicks. This guy better have some posh assignments or I'm coming right back home where my bed is warm and the pints are cold.

Las Vegas

Sarah pulled into Brian's driveway and scowled when she saw Vince's truck. *What the hell? Why didn't he put that in storage?*

Her stomach turned as she strode up the front walk.

What's going on here? Maybe he changed his mind?

She opened the door and saw all the familiar faces. Blue-eyed and distinguished, Will Adams, the team's moral compass and the supply genius who made silk purses out of sows' ears for every mission they had. He was the ranking member of the team and the man in charge now. Brian Allen, the long, lean Texan and ex Navy SEAL with stunningly sharp features and velvet brown eyes was the man they always depended upon to blow shit up on time. If he wasn't on the clock, you could find him at the nearest pool or the nearest babe. He'd be in both of them eventually. Jason Williams, with his curly brown hair and Cheshire cat grin, was the man who took care of all the team's weapons needs. He was young and acted pretty stupid, but if you gave him a knife and a block of wood, he'd give you an operational firearm in about ten minutes. He had an insane streak and that made him very dangerous if anyone crossed him. He always had Sarah's back and it made her safe in the midst of chaos. Christopher "Chris" Wilson III was the team's communications man who could chat up women in at least seven languages and had done so on several occasions. He was a fish out of water in a tactical situation, but plug him into a radio he'd tell you shit you'd never imagine. And Vince...

"Vince?"

He scooped her into his arms.

"Oh my god, you changed your mind? What happened? Is Nikolai..."

He kissed her deep and long but something was wrong.

She pulled away.

"Hey, why stop now? Let's go get a room." Vince was speaking, but it wasn't his voice.

"What the hell?" She pulled away from the stranger with the familiar face.

"Expecting somebody else?" A wide grin cut across his face.

"You're Rig, aren't you?"

"We should be sure. I don't like to leave room for error." He grabbed her, catching her off guard by dipping her backwards, and kissed her again.

What the hell, he's Vince's brother. Why would a man treat his brother's girlfriend this way? She tried to take a breath but his mouth was overpowering hers.

I can't hurt him. That wouldn't go over well in the way of first impressions. He ran his hand up her thigh, her ribs and then cupped her breast.

Fuck it! I don' care who this bastard is, he's gone way too far.

Sarah pulled the hidden knife from under her belt and pressed the blade to his neck.

He stopped kissing her but didn't move. His eyes opened wide, his pupils dilated.

She pushed the blade against his skin. One flick of her wrist and Vince wouldn't have a twin. He was still close so she spoke softly as she glared into eyes only inches from hers. "Get your fucking hands off me before I eliminate Vince's status as a twin."

He slowly set her right so both feet were on the floor and then took a step away. He kept a smile on his face though the knife stayed at his neck.

Sarah moved the knife from his throat and wiped her mouth with the back of her free hand, suppressing the urge to spit.

"Apparently your mother neglected to teach you manners, Anthony Hennessee."

His eyes sparkled. "After what we just did, you can leave Mom out of this."

The nerve of this guy.

Fury boiled Sarah's blood and she gritted her teeth. She slid the knife back into its hidden scabbard under her belt and threw a hard punch directly at Rig's face.

He caught her fist in mid flight.

Sarah caught her breath,

He was definitely expecting that.

Every pound of force she'd thrown into the punch came ricocheting back into her rage.

"Nice touch but Gina gave me a heads up on your swing. I'll have to thank her for that."

"Bastard."

"Hey, girlie, save the spunk for the bedroom because this really isn't how you should welcome a member of the family."

Asshole.

"I see. And copping a feel off your brother's girlfriend is all right?"

He shrugged and smiled. "It is if she's hot and not his wife."

Sarah turned toward the door. "If it weren't so completely fucked up, I'd consider that flattery."

"Don't trouble yourself. You're way too bossy for my taste. I like a woman who knows her place. Vince always was a pussy. He's always liked the bossy ones."

"Will, we've got work to do in the morning and I'm not in the mood for this shit today. I'm out of here." Sarah reached for the door.

Will stepped in front of her. He half winced, half smiled at her. "Can't let you do that, Sarah. Word leaked Vince was back in country so we need the twin. You're going to have to stay and make nice with the new guy on the team."

19

"The new guy? What are you talking about? Just because he looks like Vince doesn't mean he can perform like Vince."

"Hey, I'm sure I can perform a whole lot better. Why don't you try me and we can get a professional's opinion."

What he said registered in Sarah's mind and flipped a switch she never knew she had.

Red. Everything is red. Die. He must die now.

She spun around and lunged at Rig but Jason, who outweighed her by about fifty pounds of pure muscle, tackled her to the floor before she could destroy the familiar, now sickening face.

Jason held her down for a moment. "Don't do it, Sarah."

Sarah took a deep breath and growled at Jason. "I'll kill him."

"We need to make this work." Jason helped her up. "He's in." He spoke slowly. "We need to accept it."

"Bullshit! Does Vince know about this?"

Jason nodded. "He set it up."

"He *what*? He never said anything to me. Come on! They may look alike but they're not interchangeable. This guy doesn't know what we do. He's of no use to us. He's a liability."

"You're right. You're right, Sarah, but he looks like Vince so he makes great bait for somebody trying to kill Vince."

She shook her head. "That's crazy." Sarah looked at Rig. "And you're all right with being bait?"

Rig shot her a smarmy smile. "Looks like you ain't the only honey pot now, don't it sugar?" He looked her over appraisingly and stopped mid-way. "Is that...?" He pointed at the ring on her left hand. "Is that from Vince?"

Sarah looked at the sparkling diamond. "Yeah, but I've decided to pass if it means holidays with you."

I'll be damned if I tell this son of a bitch it isn't going to happen.

Rig turned away from Sarah. "Whatev'. . . more pumpkin pie for me. Have you considered Vince might have wanted to get away from you?"

She glared at him. "What's that supposed to mean?" She regretted the words as soon as they'd escaped her lips. She'd taken Rig's bait.

"Well, his last attempt at marriage didn't go so well. Maybe he decided he'd rather take on the Russian Mafia singlehandedly than hang around here with you." He shrugged. "Just sayin'."

Sarah closed her eyes hard, breathed deep and imagined flying into him from behind with her fist going through the back of his head.

Get a grip, Sarah.

Will stopped him. "All right, that's enough. Rig you're way outa line."

"*I'm* outa line? Tell me why a career Marine has to take shit from a friggin' Air Force cop who couldn't make weight? While you're at it tell me why the God damned Central Intelligence Agency, which has been assassinating assholes since day one, can't get their shit together long enough to put a hit on a fuckin' gangster and finish the job. Then tell me why my brother is out there with nobody to cover his six. You guys are all wasted on this job, and her, Jesus! She's the biggest fucking joke of all. This whole thing is fucked. Get me a beer, bitch."

"You son of a…"

Brian and Jason both turned toward Rig and slammed him into the wall, holding him there.

Chris whispered in Sarah's ear as he placed his hands firmly on her shoulders. "Don't do it, Sarah. He's being a douche but you need to hold that temper in check."

Brian snarled at Rig. "Lock it up, man. We aren't gonna stand for any more of this shit from you."

"Maybe you don't understand how important this is but we'll be happy to pound it into your head if we need to." Jason growled.

Sarah saw her chance and tried to shake free of Chris' grip.

His voice was soft. "Can't let you do that, sweetheart."

Will stepped forward and got into Rig's face. "Listen to me and listen good. If it weren't for that so-called joke over there, you and your entire platoon would have been blown to bits on August nineteenth at three in the morning when your camp got hit with heavy mortar fire and one-hundred-thirty members of Al Qaeda lit up your asses with rockets and fifty-caliber machine guns."

"Bullshit. There was no such attack." He wriggled to free himself from the vice created by Jason, Brian and the wall. "Get off me."

Jason and Brian each took a cautious step back, ready to pounce again if necessary.

Will didn't move an inch. "That's right. There was no such attack because Sarah got the intel when nobody else could, and the fucking CIA put a stop to the attack by blowing the shit out of Al Qaeda's cave." He grabbed Rig's chin, aiming his gaze toward Sarah, and pointed to her with his free hand. "That fucking joke over there is the reason you're alive and bitching so if I were you I'd take a deep borrowed breath, thank her for the extremely hard work she's done and start showing some respect before I let these boys give you a complimentary attitude adjustment." Will turned to walk away but stopped, turned on his heel, and glared at Rig. "And just so we're clear, you're the fucking new guy here so you go get Stevens a beer, bitch."

Yeah, bitch.

Three

New York

Vince checked his watch. It was going to be a long series of flights from Las Vegas to Moscow. Maybe he should have given Sarah some warning about what a dickhead Rig could be. He shrugged off the thought.

Sarah's tough. She can handle him. Besides, Rig may be stupid but he knows what's at stake here and he's smart enough not to jeopardize this mission.

He knew he could trust his brother when it came to something as important as this.

I hope he doesn't piss her off. That could start things badly. I'll give her a call from New York in the morning and see how it went.

Las Vegas

The phone on Sarah's nightstand rang.

Vince's ring.

Sarah sprung upright in bed, picked up the phone and pressed the answer button. "You son of a bitch!"

"Well, good morning to you too, sweetheart. I guess you met Rig?"

Sarah gripped the phone like a vise. If she could have reached through the phone and strangled Vince, she would have. "Don't even think about *sweethearting* me! Have I met him? He's intimately familiar with my left breast if that's what you mean by met."

"He didn't."

"Oh, yes, he did. I thought you'd changed your mind and decided to stay. How could you not tell me about this? Do you know how stupid I felt when I was the only person who wasn't in on the joke?"

"Aw, shit."

"Aw, shit is right. Next time you think about setting me up, you'd better think again because it doesn't end well."

"I'm sorry. I figured he'd be on his best behavior."

"He is now."

"What happened?"

"There was a knife involved."

"Jesus, Sarah! Did you cut him?"

"No, he's your brother. I wouldn't cut him but I sure as hell wanted to. Jason, Brian and Will had a little 'come to Jesus' meeting with him though."

"It came to that?"

"Hey, he had delusions of grandeur and thought I was his own personal beer wench, though that wasn't the word he used."

Vince groaned. "That stupid son of a bitch."

"Vince, I know he's your brother so I mean no disrespect toward you or the rest of your family but..."

"I know, baby. He's a dickhead."

"Okay, just so we're clear on that."

"Crystal clear. "So other than that, is everything okay?"

"Yeah, we're being briefed this morning so we'll see if he can pull his head out of his ass long enough to keep it together in front of Young."

"All right. I'll give him a call. Take care of yourself."

Already he's giving me "Take care of yourself"? That didn't take long.

Sarah swallowed her ego over their quickly changed relationship status. One minute she was "baby" and the next it was "take care of yourself". It seemed Vince hadn't quite made the adjustment. "You too."

Vince's line went dead. She had a feeling he was about to rip Rig a new asshole and she wished she could be on the line for it.

Hopefully he can set Rig straight so he doesn't fuck this operation, both of these operations, up.

New York

Vince didn't give Rig a chance to say hello. "You stupid son of a bitch!"

"What? Who is this?"

"Who the hell do you think?" Every fiber of his being wanted to reach through the phone and strangle his idiot twin.

"Hi, bro. What's up?"

"What's up? Your head up your ass is what! You groped Sarah?"

"Hey, she wanted it."

Vince's skin crawled like a million angry ants were trying to find a way in. "She thought you were me, dickhead." The idea of anyone else touching Sarah made him crazy. He thought he could deal with the work she did but the truth was he couldn't. The fact that his brother was the latest offender only made it all that much worse.

"Well, whose fault is that?" Rig laughed. "I can't believe you put a rock on her finger and then didn't bother to tell her you were dropping me into the operation. That doesn't say much for your relationship."

Damnit. The diamond. He may be right but I'll be damned if I confirm it.

"Shut the fuck up, Rig. Just shut your fucking mouth right now." Vince took a deep breath and tried to stay calm. His hand clenched in the same grip he wished he had on Rig's neck right now. He'd be kicking himself for a long time for how he handled things with Sarah, but that was none of Rig's business. "Rig, you're the last person on earth to be giving me relationship advice. I'm telling you right now, you treat her and everyone else on that team with the appropriate respect due to people with way more operational experience and rank than you."

"Hey, hold on a minute. They don't have..."

Vince didn't let him finish. "I'm serious, Rig. This is life and death shit. If you fuck it up because you think you're God's gift to life, the universe and everything, so help me I'll hunt you down like a dog and beat you so hard you'll wish you were dead. This isn't a game, asshole. This is the real deal and it's real fucking dangerous. Don't screw it up."

"Aw, bro. Don't get mad. It was all in fun."

Vince didn't want to hear it. They couldn't afford any errors on this operation. "Too late. You've got a briefing today. Pull your head out of your ass and get there early with Will."

Vince hung up before Rig could give him any lame stories about why he was so incompetent.

C.I.A. Training Camp Outside Las Vegas

Young walked into the briefing room and set a stack of folders on the conference table. "Good morning. I trust everyone is refreshed and feeling fine after their extended vacations. We'll save the 'what I did during my vacation in Saudi Arabia' essays for another day."

Everyone around the table, except for Rig, averted their gazes and said nothing. Sarah and the rest of the team had known there would be a good chance the Agency would find out about their hostage rescue, but they had hoped Young wouldn't call them on it. Sarah said a silent prayer for a change in subject.

"Stevens, how's that gunshot wound you got in Italy?"

Sarah stretched her arm above her head, rolled her shoulder and smiled. "Good as new."

"Good. Glad to see that retirement thing didn't pan out." Young turned and popped a K-cup in the Keurig coffee maker in the corner of the room and pushed the brew button. The machine hissed softly as he continued. "Did you get everything settled with that estate you inherited in Italy? Damned impressive how you got a foreign attaché to name you his beneficiary. We definitely picked the right woman for the job if you could get an Italian you just met to leave you everything in his will."

What a prick. "Oh, yeah. No problems at all. As it happens, there was a distant cousin who had been chomping at the bit to get Angelo's estate for years." *That's my story and I'm sticking to it. Young and the rest of the agency don't need to know Elisabetta Scuro, the "distant cousin", is actually my alias.*

Young grabbed the freshly brewed Columbian blend and turned to face Sarah, grinning, before taking a drink of his coffee.

"Fine. We don't need our agents saddled with running multi-million dollar estates when they're undercover."

Is that a twinge of jealousy in your voice?

Sarah smiled her smarmiest. "Absolutely not."

Young eyed Sarah as he took another sip. "You sure you want to keep doing this job? You could do all right as someone's Sugar Baby."

Three douchebags in three days. I'm on a roll when it comes to assholes in my life.

Sarah eyed Young and didn't flinch. "That's why Uncle Sam pays me the big bucks, Colonel."

Second time in two days I've been dissed by an over-muscled prick.

"You either have a death wish or you've got guts." He shrugged. "Most agents would cash in their chips and retire. I know I would."

Most agents aren't hard core bitches.

"I'm not most agents, Sir, but anytime you need a lesson on how to be a Sugar Baby, you just let me know."

The tension broke when Rig laughed so hard he snarfed coffee through his nose and onto the table.

"Hennessee, you all right?" Young seemed almost relieved to have the break in the conversation. It had been going sideways fast and Sarah's temper was reaching for the red zone. Young looked around the table taking a visual inventory of the team. The hairs on the back of Sarah's neck stood up.

Rig is never going to pull this off. Vince and Young have worked together too long.

Rig looked down at the table. "Yes, Sir. Just peachy."

Young cocked his head. "The shrinks cleared you. Something you can't leave in the past?"

"Let's just say my vacation wasn't as restful as I'd expected." Rig rubbed his palms together. "But it's all good."

Young squinted at him.

It's over. Rig talked too much.

"Okay, let's get on with the briefing, shall we?" Young set his coffee cup on the table and pulled a remote from his cargo pocket. A projector mounted to the ceiling switched on and a map of Europe and Asia popped up on the wall behind him.

Jason rubbed his hands together, feigning excitement. "Ooh! Visual aids!"

Young rolled his eyes and continued. "As you all know, we've been working for some time to get Afghanistan on its feet and get farmers producing legal crops instead of the poppy crops they've been producing since the Taliban was eliminated from the picture."

"Ninety-three percent of the world's opium," Chris added.

Young nodded. "That's coming into the United States as various forms of Heroin and causing quite a mess. Now they're cutting it with a synthetic form of heroin and practically doubling their money. Needless to say, it has become a major cash crop and the people cashing in are the insurgents and Al Qaeda. The bastards causing us to be there in the first place."

"It's a vicious, lucrative cycle." Chris nodded.

"Yes, it is. That's why we're assigning you to stop it."

"Whoa. Why us?" Will seemed surprised by the assignment. "That isn't our area of operations or expertise. We've got other teams over there. Doesn't White Wolf have that area covered?"

Young shook his head. "Generally speaking, yes, they would cover that area but since the Red Wolf team was taken out, White Wolf has been called into Russia to work on that case."

Brian didn't look happy. "Okay, so we're working the *Stans* now?"

"Don't worry, Allen. You'll still be near water. We have an asset who's been helping us in Tangiers. She's going to walk you through the business end of things out there." Young walked around the table and dropped file folders in front of each team member.

They began flipping through them.

"Your job on this mission is to set Stevens up as an import/export specialist, a dealer of sorts. She'll be working with Giselle, our asset, on that operation and you all will need to back her up. This isn't a trailer park operation.

Stevens needs to be set up well to look like she's very important and has a large organization. The cover story will be she's buying out Giselle. Giselle will make the appropriate introductions to key players but it's your team's job to map as much of the organization as possible. Like every one of your operations, this has to be top shelf."

Sarah interrupted. "Hold on a minute. It's one thing to be placed as arm candy on an observation post, but what you're saying sounds like I'm taking point on this. I hope I'm wrong."

Young shook his head. "No. You're right. Is that a problem?"

"But Will's got the experience..."

Young interrupted Sarah. "Will's a seasoned agent but you've got more missions left in you. I expect we'll be seeing Will retiring next. Everybody has to start somewhere. It's time to step up, Stevens. Can you handle it?"

Sarah held back a smile and her heartbeat quickened. This was the best news she'd had in days. Being able to focus completely on work and busting bad guys would take her mind of her sad excuse for a personal life.

Holy shit.

"Yeah. Let's do it."

Young continued with the briefing. "Major Hennessee and I spoke yesterday. He's informed me that this will be his last mission and he will serve in an advisory role only while Master Chief Adams takes over as team leader. Major Hennessee assured me you were all on board with that plan. Is that correct? Are all of you okay with that?"

"Oh, yeah." Brian nodded.

Jason closed the dossier in front of him. "Good plan."

Chris looked up. "I am."

Sarah sat back in her chair and glowered at Rig. "Yeah, we're all on board."

Four

Las Vegas

Sarah sat alone on the couch at Brian's. Everyone else was standing around the barbeque grill watching the master griller, Brian, work on their usual post-briefing steaks.

Will walked into the kitchen and grabbed a beer from the refrigerator. "You want one, pork chop?"

She smiled at the pet name he used for her, a remnant from her overweight past. "No, thanks."

"How about a shot of tequila? Brian brought in a new label from Texas called 'Source of all Happiness'." He chuckled.

Sarah smiled a weak smile. "Nah. Not a good idea today."

"What's going on in that head of yours, Sarah?" He walked around the bar to the living room and sat next to her on the couch.

Sarah shook her head. "I could be living the dream. I could have had plastic surgery, changed my hair color and disappeared forever on the money I have now. You and Vince could have done the same. None of us are hurting for money. We could have all cashed in our chips and been living the good life right now."

Jason walked in and sat on the other side of Sarah. "This IS the good life, sweetheart!"

"Let's cut the bull. You and Vince have a certain bond. There's no denying that. Thing is, we all go solo at some point and it does no good for any of us to worry about the other when we've got our own work to take care of." Will pulled a cigar from his pocket.

Leave it to Will to cut to the chase.

"Of course the distance bothers me. Where is he? Is he all right? If something happens to him, will we even know? Hell, Young didn't even tell us when Vince was kidnapped by Nikolai. At the briefing, he acted like it never happened."

Jason cracked open his beer and took a drink before putting his arm around Sarah. "Do you know what your problem is?"

Sarah looked sideways at him. "Why don't you tell me, Jase?"

"You love the thought of being in love but it gets in the way of who you really are. You're not wired like other women."

She snickered at the irony of it. "Gee, thanks."

"No, wait a minute." He placed his beer on the coffee table, grabbed the pack of Marlboro Reds resting there, and flipped a cigarette from the pack into his mouth. "Think about it." He lit the cigarette and snapped his lighter closed with a flick of his wrist. "You love the idea of love, home, hearth and that white picket fence, but if you aren't kicking ass on a daily basis you don't feel alive. Am I right?"

Sarah tried to shrug it off and didn't answer but what he said made complete sense.

He's got me.

"Sarah, if I didn't spar with you full out every day you'd be busting up bars just for kicks. I may be a Green Beret but it ain't easy rolling out of bed some days when I know I have to face you in the ring. Are you gonna tell me you can be happy in suburbia with spinning class and carpooling the kids to soccer practice?"

The cold truth hit like a punch in the face.

Jesus, he's right. I know that's what Vince wants but it isn't me. Not anymore.

Sarah tried to inject some levity. "Well look at you, Jason!" She smiled. To think I thought you were just another pretty face."

"I'm just sayin' Vince is a big boy and can take care of himself. He knew what he was getting into and so do we. We live day to day on this gig. We don't have the luxury of time to worry about what's going on with other agents. Get over it."

Will crossed his right ankle over his left knee. "The boy's got a point."

Sarah took a deep breath and sighed. Jason was right. She'd been holding on to some outdated "stand by your man" mentality when in fact, she needed to start thinking like a true CIA Agent. If she were honest with herself, she'd have to admit she loved being engrossed in the excitement and the power in the job she did.

"You've got a point." She nodded. "As much as I hate to admit it, I like the action. I thrive on the high speed lifestyle even though I never suspected I would. Why don't relationships ever work out for agents though? I've heard about couples who worked together during the cold war."

Will took a drink. "They're anomalies. Love will make you bleed. One way or another it'll get you."

Jason stood. "It's the curse of the super hero." He flashed his Cheshire cat grin and walked back out to the patio.

~~~

Sarah dropped the dossier on the kitchen table where she had been drinking coffee and studying while the guys played video games. "Will, what's the deal with Giselle Dumais? How do I fit in here?"

Will folded the Wall Street Journal he'd been reading and set it neatly on the side table by the leather recliner everyone acknowledged as his domain. "You and she are business associates."

Sarah sighed. " At least I don't have to sleep my way to the top this time." She grinned. "Okay, talk to me. How is this going to work?"

"Short story is you're a drug dealer."

Sarah's stomach rolled. She knew Will and Vince had posed as arms dealers, hell, they'd *been* arms dealers for years now but she hated the idea of selling drugs to anyone. After all she'd done in the line of duty she'd still have some difficulty jumping this moral hurdle.

"Better give me the long story, Will. I know I've done a lot of bad things but I'm not sure I can do this one. Besides, I'm a lousy saleswoman."

"It's all about the acting. You're a great actress when you want to be and this assignment is no different than any of the others."

She lit a cigarette and shook her head. "Not the way I see it."

"Every mission we take happens in some moral no-man's land. This is no different. You're posing as an international businesswoman who specializes in import and export. You won't be sampling, cutting or coming into any contact with actual drugs. You're the boss. You call the shots. You make the deals. You have an organization of hundreds to do the dirty work. You're the CEO."

She set her cigarette on the edge of the ash tray and squinted at Will. "You think I can pull off CEO?"

"Don't worry. That's why you've got me and the knuckle draggers over there."

Chris looked up from the video game appearing hurt. "Hey now! I'm evolved."

Brian and Jason focused on the game.

Will shrugged and turned back to Sarah. "Have I steered you wrong yet?"

Sarah grinned. "No, you haven't. Okay, where do we start?"

"Let's look at your first assignment. Hassan. He was the boss. He ran his organization of hundreds from that yacht. You never saw the whole organization. What did you see?"

"His secretary and his bodyguards."

"That's right." Will nodded. "In this case, your secretary will always be a phone call away. Let's call him Chris." Will smiled.

"Okay, that makes sense. So which one of the guys is going to be my bodyguard?"

"Here's where it gets tricky. I've got a price on my head, Rig is wearing Vince's face, Brian needs to skipper the boat, Jason needs to be our go-to and gofer and Chris, well, I think you'll agree when I say Chris is no bodyguard. Hell, he can barely get to the bathroom without hurting himself."

Chris shouted over the game noise. "Hey, I resent that!"

Sarah laughed.

"What's great is you've been orbiting in the right circles to make this look real. It would be easy enough for you to have picked up a few tricks and seed money from the men you've been involved with to start your own business. Maybe you hooked up with a guy who staked you in this enterprise. That's not a bad idea. We could roll with that."

"Great. We've got a back story but I still need some muscle to look legit. We haven't got anyone we can use here and we can't use anybody from the agency because of the Vince/Rig situation. Do I go in alone?"

"Hell no. You'll look like an amateur if you don't have quality muscle."

"So where do we get it?"

Will smiled like he knew something she didn't. "You'll hire a bodyguard like any other businessman would. We'll outsource. We'll call Brock Benjamin."

"This is a bodyguard gig, Will. I need a guy I can take out in public, not some nameless mercenary like his guys we used in Saudi. We can't outsource spy work."

"Not the spy work, just the bodyguard. We put in a call to a guy we can trust and we buy you some primo muscle."

Sarah raised a brow and flashed a naughty grin. "Okay, I'm liking the sound of that."

Jason set down his game controller. "Hey, how come she gets to buy a hottie but we can't?"

"Because she's the boss." Will directed his attention back to Sarah. "Brock owns Sentrion Services. Check it out some time. It's huge. Brock is the guy the heads of state and Hollywood hot-shots call for bodyguards."

Will picked up Sarah's phone from the table and tapped a number into it. "That's Brock's personal number. Tell him who you are. I'll put money on it he's heard about you. The less he knows the better but tell him everything you want in a bodyguard and I guarantee he'll have the guy we need within twenty-four hours."

"That quickly?"

"Brock's the best."

Sarah shook her head. "Apparently." She put the phone to her ear just as Brock answered.

"Brock Benjamin."

"Hi, Brock. My name's Sarah Stevens."

"The beautiful, elusive, and infamous Miss Stevens. I've been hoping you'd call."

She smiled. "Oh, really? Why?"

"Just so I could hear the voice of a hard driving, tequila drinking, knife throwing, badass with cojones the size of Mexico City and a set of knockers that... well, maybe I shouldn't repeat that part. Trust me, it's all good. What can I do for you?"

"I need a bodyguard."

"You? You've got the skills to *be* one. Quit that gig and I'll get you a personal protection job in a heartbeat."

"Uh, thanks, I'll keep that in mind. But I like this job and I really do need a bodyguard. I'll be doing some international work that requires an intimidation factor."

"Okay, you tell me what you need in a bodyguard and I'll find her for you."

"Let's make it a him, please?"

"Testicles, check."

"For obvious reasons, I need a guy who can keep his mouth shut. He should have tactical driving experience. He needs to be good with weapons but just as strong with hand-to-hand combat since we'll be in and out of commercial airports. He's got to have a cool head."

"Sarah, that's all standard bodyguard stuff. What's unique to you?"

Sarah took a deep breath and exhaled. "He should be able to dress well and not look like a trained monkey with a tie. He'll need to wear business suits daily, no JC Penney suits or combat boots. He's got to be class. He'll be expected to escort me to formal functions and needs to be fit. I've got standards. I don't wear Louboutins on the arm of a slob."

"You sure you don't want to call Hardbody Escorts instead of me?"

"Can you do this, Brock, or are we wasting our time here?"

"Yeah, you are a hardass." Brock laughed. "I'm just kidding. What else do you need?"

"Versatility. We'll be traveling a lot. Someone up on world events so I don't have to explain everything to him. I'd feel more comfortable with somebody with military experience. Former special forces is a plus. He should have a working knowledge of Russian too." Sarah exhaled. "Is there such an animal?"

"You sure you don't have any other requests? Height, build, eye color, facial hair, hairstyle? If I didn't feel like I already know you, I'd feel kinda dirty setting this up."

Sarah rolled her eyes. "Great. Now I see why Guinea spoke so highly of you." Guinea Man, alias Anthony Gilbert, was a friend of Vince's and a former agent who'd been burned and, after a short stay on Vince's private island off Dubai, created a new life for himself by going to work for Brock Benjamin, his former partner in The Agency. She'd heard stories about Brock, but this was her first conversation with him.

"Hey, I can send you Guinea."

"No way. His hair's too long."

Brock chuckled. "I made him get a haircut. That long look isn't popular with the clients."

Sarah sighed. "On behalf of women everywhere, thank you. So can you do this?"

"Piece of cake. Where and when?"

Sarah gave Brock the details and they set up the transfer of funds for the initial payment.

Sarah hung up the phone and smiled. "I like that guy."

Five

Charlotte, North Carolina

Brock Benjamin leaned forward in the soft leather chair at his huge oak desk, his starched white shirt open at the neck, and his brown silk tie tossed haphazardly on a small stack of file folders. He examined his receding hairline from every angle with the small drugstore hand mirror. "I'm telling you, honey. My hairline looks exactly like the Eastern seaboard now."

A calm, low, woman's voice came through the speakerphone on his desk. "Brock, you own the largest private military company in the Western Hemisphere…"

"No, technically, no." Brock pointed at the phone for a moment before going back to his hairline. "There's that other company. They're under a decade of indictments but they haven't been liquidated yet."

"My point, dearest, is that you handle millions of dollars in government contracts and God knows how many more in private contracts every year and you're spending the morning examining your hairline?"

"Well, yeah." Brock set the mirror down and shrugged. "I have people to handle all those contracts."

"Well, I don't have people and I'm in the middle of a real estate deal so why don't you spend some of your spare time thinking of a nice place to take me to dinner tonight?"

Brock picked up the mirror again and rubbed his chin. "You think I should grow a beard?"

The intercom buzzed. "Mr. Stanstead is here to see you."

Brock pushed the intercom button. "Great, send him in." He tucked the mirror into his top desk drawer. "Gotta go, honey. I can't sit around gabbing with you on the phone all morning." He pushed the button to end the call, pushed his tie aside and grabbed the file folders that rested in a neat stack to his left just as Jay Stanstead knocked on his open office door.

Brock smiled and waved him in. "Jay, come on in. You did a great job on the King's security detail last week. They were all very impressed with you."

Jay looked the ideal candidate for the Stevens gig. He wore a grey silk suit with a black T-shirt that macho'd it up a bit. He was in his late thirties but still hard as a rock from twenty years with the Special Air Service. Brock didn't know what type Sarah Stevens went for but Jay didn't appear to be the kind of guy who had to work hard to find women.

"Thanks, Brock. I'm glad they were pleased. It was a nice job. Clean conditions, good meals, private jets. I wouldn't mind more like that."

Brock smiled. "I'm glad to hear you say that. I got a call from a very important client this morning. I've got a personal security job I would like you to take a look at."

"Sure, Brock." Jay nodded. "I'll take a look."

Brock stood and walked around the desk toward a side door in his office. He opened the door and grinned. "Come on into the conference room. This is the job of a lifetime and I've got a couple other guys who are interested too."

Brock followed Jay into the conference room where two other men were waiting.

~~~

Jay Stanstead had spent his career in the British Army's Special Air Service (SAS) jumping out of planes, cutting more throats than he cared to count, and drinking more pints than he could remember. He'd invested his money well and had a comfortable retirement courtesy of the crown, but his life was missing something he couldn't live without--action.

On the suggestion of his comrade, Ian Urquhart, he met with Brock Benjamin, the owner of a private military company that specialized in freelance work for guys with a certain type of military experience--Jay's type of military experience. Jay enjoyed the first personal security job Brock had given him and earned a few great recommendations in just one week.

Today, Brock's secretary called him in to the office for a meeting with Brock. As he walked into Brock's conference room, he nodded hello to the two other men there. Apparently all three of them would be taking a look at a special job.

"Have a seat, guys." Brock handed them each a file folder. "Go ahead and take a look at the job."

Jay opened the folder to find an eight-by-ten photo of the most stunning woman he'd ever laid eyes on. No woman, real or photographed, had ever made Jay's heart stop--until today.

Barry let out a loud wolf whistle from across the table. "I'll take a piece of that!"

Jose, the third man, smiled. "Ay, mami! I'll do the job without pay if I get to do her."

"A little respect, boys. This woman could kick your asses six ways to Sunday and she's responsible for my last quarter's earnings climbing twenty percent. She's an international businesswoman and needs a personal security specialist, a bodyguard, not a man whore."

Jay wanted this client. He had to have this client. The job description was like a dream. The pay was excellent and the conditions were guaranteed first class. "I'll take it."

"Whoah, whoah!" Barry glared at Brock.

Jose glanced at Barry and Jay. "So do we all get the job?"

Brock stood and grinned wide. "I called all three of you in this morning because you're my best men. This is a big job and I know you're all coming off high-profile jobs so here it is: Ms. Scuro is in the import/ export business and flies into some rough places. She needs a guy who looks like she belongs on his arm but can handle any rough stuff in the more male dominated countries. Travel is generally by private jet but some commercial travel may be necessary. You'll be armed as necessary. The budget on this job is huge and the length of the assignment is indefinite."

Jay squinted at Brock. "So which one of us gets the job?"

Brock smiled. "Alas, there can be only one. You men go ahead and figure it out amongst yourselves who is going to take the job. I'll expect to see one of you in my office in ten minutes." He left the room and closed the door behind him.

Jay glanced at the other two men and stood. "Sorry, mates. I'll be taking this one."

Jose stood. "No way, man. A cool little number like that and first class. You'll take it over my dead body." He moved toward the door.

Jay stepped between Jose and the door and smiled. "Sorry, mate."

Jose seemed confused. "You wouldn't."

Jay threw an uppercut that launched Jose back into the room, where he landed in a heap on the floor.

Barry stood slowly from his chair at the table. He raised his hands in surrender. "The job's all yours, bro."

Moscow

Vince stepped into the limousine and the driver closed the door softly before standing, arms crossed behind him, outside the door as any bodyguard should. Vince smiled a greeting to Mark and Buffy Davidson who were waiting inside on the bench seat across from the open door. "Hi, guys. Nice ride." He took a seat across the aisle in the stretch limo.

Mark smiled and tipped his head to indicate it was Buffy's idea.

Buffy bubbled and pulled her sable coat around her shoulders to shield her from the cold winter air that came in with Vince. "Hi, Vince. How's Sarah?"

Buffy reminded Vince too much of his ex wife, all bubbly blonde and big boobs. To Vince's relief, Mark spoke quickly. "I have to make this fast, Vince. We have a dinner to get to."

Buffy pulled out a compact and checked her lipstick.

Vince tried not to be distracted by Buffy's ample cleavage spilling from the deep neckline of her dress as the sable slipped down her shoulders. "Okay. No problem."

"Angelica Leonova has a small apartment waiting for you." He passed Vince an index card with an address on it. "Don't get excited. It's one room and a three quarter bathroom."

Vince took the card and read the address. "What's the connection?"

Davidson grinned. "It's a beauty. She's the long time mistress of Mikhail Andreovich Drugov. He used to be the leader of the Mikhailovich family but he's retired now. He's old school *vor y zakone*."

"That's the red mafia, right?"

Mark nodded. "Yeah, it used to be. The lines have blurred now but his son, also old school *vor*, has brought the family into the twenty-first century with some very legit-looking investments. It's all to wash the money, of course, but it makes them look more like businessmen and bankers than gangsters."

"I'm still looking for the connection, Mark."

"It turns out Nikolai is a boss in a rival group who pissed in Mikhailovich Jr.'s Cheerios one too many times and junior is hot to see him brought down."

"So I'm supposed to suck up to the old man?"

"No. Not that easy, I'm afraid. That's the last thing you want to do. He's old school so he'll be impressed by the basics like how stand-up a guy you are, how helpful you are to Angelika. Stuff like that." Mark tugged on his cuffs. "I'm not gonna lie. It'll take some time. They don't readily trust outsiders."

"Understandable." Vince nodded. "So I make nice with the old lady, she'll bring the old man along and then he'll bring the son along."

"That is the idea, yes."

"Geez, Mark, next time make the trail a little less direct, huh?"

"Hey, it's a crooked road but it gets us where we want to go without being too obvious."

"Yeah, yeah."

Buffy snapped her compact shut and raised her perfectly plucked brows at Mark. "We have a timetable."

Mark pulled an envelope from his breast pocket and handed it to Vince.

"I can't drop you in that neighborhood in this car. Here's some cash for a taxi." Vince fingered through the bundle of rubles. "That'll do more than pay for a taxi."

"You might need a little something to flash. Just take it. I'll be in touch as soon as I have more information for you." He reached over and shook Vince's hand. "Good luck."

"Thanks, Mark." He nodded to Buffy. "Buffy, always a pleasure to see you."

She smiled. "And you! Take care of yourself."

Las Vegas

Sarah made her way to one of the reclining chairs in the back of the jet and set her carry-on on the floor by her feet. The number of periodicals she had to subscribe to in order to stay on top of world events and international society made for heavy bags these days.

"Hey, honey." Rig flopped into the high-backed, leather seat next to Sarah. He had a ridiculous grin on his face.

Sarah sighed.

He looks so much like Vince but acts like such a jerkoff. How can I love the face and hate what's inside? How can I possibly work with this guy and not think about Vince constantly?

She smiled at him and put her forefinger to her lips. "Shh...Don't talk. Just sit there and look pretty."

He tipped his head like a dog who'd just heard his name, and didn't say a word.

Sarah grinned with self-satisfaction and opened a magazine. She tried to read but couldn't focus so she set her issue of Foreign Affairs on the side table and stretched, glancing across the aisle at Will.

He must have felt her stare because he didn't even look over his newspaper. He spoke from behind it. "What?"

"Why couldn't he just let it go? Surely there are plenty of people who want us dead. Nikolai will either pop up again eventually and we can knock him off or he'll just disappear under his rock and leave us all alone. Why couldn't Vince just walk away from this one?"

Rig perked up. "Oh, I can tell you that."

Sarah turned to him, scowled, and put her finger to her lips again.

He sat back and mouthed the words "Fuck you," but he was still smiling.

"That's not the kind of guy he is, Sarah. He can't not answer the call to protect the people he cares about. That's Vince's weakness. When he's challenged, he'll take that challenge no matter what it is. Nothing and no one can stop him."

Sarah sighed. "It is an admirable quality."

"Yeah." Will lowered his paper. "It's heroic, but if you've ever read the tales of Greek heroes they always end in tragedy. Look at Hector and Andromache. Great love story, lots of passion, lots of action, but a lousy ending. He dies and she's captured and made a concubine." Will winced. "That's why we let the job make us hard. There's less tragedy."

Moscow

Vince listened carefully as the old woman spoke perfect Russian with no detectable dialect at all. "Your apartment is on the third floor. I hope you don't mind the stairs."

Though it was bitter cold in Moscow he was glad it was winter. The black knit watch cap covered his head and the leather coat hid his physique. His bald head and massive build were usually the first things to give him away. At least he'd have winter clothes to hide behind for the next few months.

That should be enough time to nail Nikolai and put him down.

"No, the stairs are fine. I like exercise." He replied in the Russian he'd learned over the years as an arms dealer. His had a slight Ukrainian accent.

"You are from Ukraine?"

Vince didn't lie. "I have spent some time there."

She kept walking up the stairs. "Do you have a job?"

"No, ma'am."

"Are you one of those Ukrainian assassins?"

Vince smiled. She was bold for an old lady. "What if I were?"

She waved a dismissive hand as she continued up the stairs. "Do not bring your work home with you." She looked down at him from the landing. "Do you use drugs?"

Vince shook his head. "No, ma'am."

She continued up the stairs. "No, you look too healthy for a drug user." She turned a fierce look on Vince from three stairs up. "You do not sell drugs from my apartment."

"No, ma'am."

"How will you pay your rent if you have no job, you're not an assassin and you don't sell drugs?"

"Cash in advance."

She stopped at the third floor landing and turned a smiling face on him. "We will get along like old friends, you and I."

Vince grinned.

I like this old broad. I like her a lot.

Vince waited for the woman to unlock the door.

When she did, he stepped into the small, clean room.

Two large windows draped with green curtains let in plenty of daylight. He guessed the single-bulb light fixture in the middle of the ceiling would make for some dreary nights. A small kitchen area to his right consisted of a refrigerator no bigger than a mini bar, a microwave, a small basin sink and a hotplate. The bathroom to his left was no more than a small hallway containing a toilet, a sink and a shower. An armoire to hold his clothes, a flat panel television, mini stereo and a queen sized bed along with a small bistro table with seating for two rounded out the room. As far as hotel rooms went, it was great. As a long-term living arrangement, it was crap.

He turned to the woman who waited by the door, just outside the room. "It is very nice, thank you." He pulled out his wallet and counted out the cash for six months rent. "Six months all right?"

"Yes, that will be fine." She grinned and shook her head. "If only all my tenants were as prompt with their rent."

"If I need it longer, I'll let you know."

"I hope you do." She smiled as she stuffed the bills into her bra. "I like how you do business."

Tangiers, Morocco

Sarah looked out the window of the private jet as they landed in Tangiers. The sun was up and promised a beautiful day. She adjusted her Rolex to eight am local time. According to their pilot, the temperature was in the mid sixties. She straightened in the leather seat and smirked. Setting down in a new place always set off tiny bubbles of excitement for her.

They landed and taxied quickly as they always did when flying into private airports. She'd come a long way from riding in jump seats of military aircraft just a few short years ago.

The crew removed their luggage and packed it into the two black Range Rovers waiting for the team on the tarmac.

After the vehicles had been checked out, Sarah stepped into the first one with Will. "Is it really necessary to always take two vehicles?"

"Standard procedure for convoys. If one gets hit, at least half the team and equipment have a shot at surviving."

"Military convoys, sure, but nobody's going to hit us here."

"We lost a team at an airport last week."

"Seriously?"

"Seriously." He nodded. "We have a lot of expensive shit we can't afford to lose either. Do you know how expensive our gear is?"

"Well, yeah. Do you know how expensive my clothes are?"

"I've seen the receipts. That wardrobe should have its own car and driver."

They drove out of the airport and into the morning traffic. A little later they pulled into a stunning complex on the coast, passing tennis courts, a golf course and carefully manicured grounds.

This would be Sarah and her bodyguard's home sweet home for the duration of the assignment in Tangiers. The team needed to minimize the possibility of Sarah being seen with Will and Rig as it would make them all less obvious targets. While Sarah was working on the official assignment, Will and the boys would also be working with Vince on the unofficial assignment, and the boat would provide them with a degree of privacy they wouldn't have if they stayed on land. The resort appeared to be first class, but she envied the boys being able to stay on a yacht just off the coast. She'd grown to love having gentle waves rock her to sleep whenever she slept on boats.

"We'll get you checked in and then head out to the boat. Jason can pick up your bodyguard at the airport after you meet with Giselle tomorrow. Then you two can move in here."

~~~

Once they'd finished loading all their gear on the yacht and Chris had swept it for bugs, Brian cast off and anchored a mile from harbor so they could set everything up in peace.

Will and Sarah walked out onto the deck and sat at the table.

Chris was already there hard at work on his laptop. "No foreign bugs in your suite, Sarah. Just mine." He grinned. "The maid is laying chocolates on your pillows. Nice ass." He sighed. "I love my job."

Sarah looked questioningly at Chris. "That was quick! You didn't even go to the hotel to set those cameras."

"I called ahead. A local agent wired it up overnight."

Will looked around. "Tomorrow's your first meeting with Giselle. You'll stay here tonight. Brian will drive you to Giselle's office and Jason will go along as your bodyguard. "When she gives you pointers, pay attention. Giselle knows what she's doing."

"What's her story? You have anything more than what's in the dossier? How's she affiliated with the agency?"

"Giselle's what's commonly referred to as an asset. She's paid for the services she renders the agency and its personnel. In this case, she's been providing intelligence and cooperation in exchange for agency protection. She's been very helpful to us, but she's getting older and doesn't travel as much as she used to. That's cutting into her ability to stay on top of what's going on in Western Asia."

So what happens when somebody like Giselle decides to retire? Does the agency just let an asset walk?

Will interrupted her thoughts. "What you need to do is become Giselle's apprentice without looking like an apprentice to her clients. You've got to hit the ground running and always look like you're on top of everything."

"I don't need to tell you that's going to be kind of difficult considering I don't know Jack about being a drug dealer."

Will shook his head. "Like I said, it isn't about being a drug dealer. We're way beyond that level. You're an international businesswoman specializing in the transportation and distribution of commodities."

She slapped her knee. "Well, hell, Will. When you put it that way, it sounds pretty cool."

He laughed. "Exactly! This is the big time, Sarah. You're a big dog now and my job, along with Giselle's, is to teach you how to bark like one." He leaned back and drew a cigar from the small leather case in his breast pocket. He pulled a trimmer and lighter from his trouser pocket and set the lighter on the table.

Sarah watched as he trimmed the cigar neatly and carefully drew breath as he lit the rich, dark, hand-rolled tobacco.

"You'll be mixing with billionaires who will either assume you're a peer or be offended that some amateur has been allowed into their inner circle."

She leaned back in the chair. "That's certainly confidence inspiring."

"I've seen you cocky and confident. You need to be all that and then some with these people."

Chris looked up from the work he was doing on his laptop. "No offense, Sarah, but I don't think this is going to work. We need a contingency plan, Will."

Whether Chris intended it or not Sarah knew this was her first test. "Chris?" She made him wait a moment while she lit a cigarette. "While I appreciate your expertise in the intelligence field, I understand that it does not always translate well to knowing what makes people tick and what heights they can rise to when challenged. Thank you. Is there coffee on in the galley?"

Chris shook his head. "I don't know."

She smiled and gave her eyelashes an extra wag. "Would you be a doll and go check?"

Chris went inside and Will stared at Sarah, a smile creeping across his face. "Now that's what I'm talking about. You do realize Chris will figure out what you just did and probably be either ashamed of himself for falling for it or offended that you did it. Either way he'll most definitely feel emasculated."

"Yeah." Sarah chuckled. "I'll just go down to the galley to make nice real quick." She stood and walked through the lounge to the galley stairs.

Chris was standing at the bottom of the stairs, glaring up at her. "You sly bitch. Do you know I had actually started brewing a pot of coffee before I realized what you just pulled on me?"

"Christopher, you of all people should know never to underestimate me. It's that constant and predictable underestimation of me by powerful men that's taken us this far." Sarah slunk down the stairs, stretching one long leg after the other for effect.

He grinned, seeming to appreciate the show. "You're right. I should have known you could do it. I'm sorry. I know you can do anything you set your mind to."

Sarah gave Chris a hug and an apologetic pout. "I'm sorry if I emasculated you."

Chris kissed her on the cheek. "That's okay." He looked up at the ceiling for a moment. "I think I just felt my balls drop again."

"Good. Now where's that coffee?"

Chris pointed to the coffee maker. "Over there. Bring me a cup when you come back up, will you?"

47

Sarah shook her head in amusement. "I'd say they dropped down bigger than before."

Chris shook his right leg and continued climbing the stairs. "Could be."

Six

Morocco

"Good morning, handsome." The elderly woman with flame red hair smiled at Jason who, in her defense, was looking particularly hot in a form fitting T-shirt and jeans. She walked directly to him and looped her arm through his, leading him to a sofa in a small sitting area in her office.

A tray with coffee and croissants waited on the coffee table.

She poured Jason a cup of coffee and only then looked at Sarah. "You must be Sarah?"

Sarah smiled, amused at the old woman fawning over Jason, and his surprise at the attention. "Yes, I am. This is my associate, Jason."

"How wonderful for you. In my experience, I only ever get to meet balding middle aged agents in cheap suits that are too tight around the tummy and never hide enough of their fat asses. But you..." She squeezed Jason's bicep and her eyes flickered with naughty flames. "You should wear as little as possible."

Jason fidgeted slightly. He seemed unused to the attention.

Sarah enjoyed watching Jason's reaction. He really was an attractive man and she never understood why he didn't get more attention from women. "You'll have to come out to the boat and visit sometime. Jason likes to swim every afternoon. He's particularly handsome in a bathing suit."

Giselle put her hand just above Jason's knee and squeezed. "I think I'd like that very much. But enough about his body, I'll look at it later. Sarah, you turn around. Let's see your ass."

It was all fun and games when Jason was being objectified, but now it was Sarah's turn. She hoped Giselle wasn't planning on a threesome. "Really?"

Giselle made a shooing motion with her red lacquered fingernails. "Turn! Turn!"

Sarah shrugged and turned around for Giselle to examine her posterior.

"Very nice. Yes, you are a very attractive woman. Don't be afraid to use it when you deal with the Russians. Buy yourself a good fur coat so you can wear short skirts. They expect women to dress like women but the Russian winters can be cold. Always wear high heels, they lift the derriere and accentuate the calves."

Sarah turned back around to face Giselle and tried desperately to keep her laughter in check.

"How are your breasts?"

"Uh..."

Jason jumped into the game with a little tit for tat. "Her breasts are spectacular."

I knew he'd been looking!

Giselle looked at him with curiosity. "You think so?"

"Yep." He nodded. "They're very nice."

Giselle pursed her lips at Jason. "Good." She directed her attention back to Sarah. "Wear blouses that are low cut but not so low the breasts fall out. We want sexy, not slutty."

Giselle leaned into Jason with her own breasts and purred her words. "Which do you prefer?"

Jason grinned. "On Sarah or just in general?"

Giselle stroked his leg. "Generally speaking."

"Personally, I like slutty. It means I have a chance."

She winked at him. "You'll have your chance. Now enough flirting. You stay here and I'll finish with her." She stood and walked over to her desk. "Let's get started with you, Sarah."

Sarah moved to a chair opposite Giselle's desk.

"These Russians you will deal with are gangsters. They understand power and strength. They're pigs too. They'd rather look at a woman than listen to her. If you look good, they'll be happy to do business with you just so they can look at you." Giselle lit a cigarette and took a long drag. "If you look better than good, they'll be distracted and let contract points slide. If you aren't willing or able to use sex appeal you're not going to get anywhere with them."

Sarah nodded. "I can do that."

Giselle leered over at Jason turning back to Sarah. "Most women want to please, and negotiate too much. That makes them look weak. Be tenacious and hold firm.

Something else that will make you look weak - not confronting people who challenge your authority." When I send you to do business and take meetings in Russia, you'll have complete authority to make any deals you like. If someone questions your authority you must be strong and unafraid to confront them on the spot. If heads deserve to roll then you need to be the one to roll them. They will respect that. Show no fear. They'll smell it like bad borscht." Giselle walked over to the sitting area, poured two cups of coffee and returned to the desk, placing one of the cups in front of Sarah.

"Thank you." Sarah took a sip of the strong black Arabic brew. Apparently Giselle didn't get enough of that from her unfiltered cigarettes.

Giselle stubbed out the red lipstick stained cigarette she had left in the ash tray.

"On the other hand, do not be put off by hand kissing, door opening and flower giving. That's how the Russians show respect. They will invite you to dinner, and it is expected that you attend but do not go out with the men after dinner. They will invite you to go drink and dance at a nightclub but you must not accept. Doing so will reduce you in their minds to a party girl and they will treat you as such." Giselle leaned across the desk, squinting as though about to conspire over some evil deed. She pointed a long red shellacked fingernail at Sarah.

"Now, listen closely. If you really want to fuck with their minds bring a hot young bodyguard like that one," she pointed at Jason who smiled his crooked smile, "and make them believe you are lovers. Are you lovers?"

Sarah chuckled. "No, we aren't. Jason is unattached."

Giselle smiled like a cougar who'd just spotted her next meal.

"Russian men don't believe a woman can be successful in business and in the bedroom. If they see that you are both, it will make them crazy for you. They'll be putty in your hands."

"But aren't they wise to this sort of manipulation?"

"Ah, Sarah. They are not only wise to it, they expect it. Business is a game to them. It is a very high stakes game but they love playing it. They especially love playing it with women who are as well equipped as you and I."

"I see."

This could be fun.

Giselle stood. "Let's go sit over there. There is so much to tell you. We should be comfortable while we talk."

Sarah stood and moved to the sofa across from Jason.

Giselle sat next to Jason and patted him on the knee before sitting back, crossing her ankles and lighting another cigarette with a long drag. "You must always try to go into every negotiation with the upper hand." She took a hard drag from the cigarette, burning it to practically half ash. "Always have a trump card. If you don't have the upper hand you're just a whore to be manipulated and those Russians will give you the business, *ma chere*." She took another long drag.

Sarah looked at the woman across from her and saw her future flash momentarily. *It may be time to quit smoking.* She understood that having the upper hand was always good, but she didn't know the first thing about working over a bunch of Russians she'd never met before and wouldn't be sleeping with. "How do I get the upper hand?"

Giselle leaned forward, her eyes opened wide. "Any way you can." She sat back. "Wear the best clothes. Make sure your bodyguard wears the best suits. Drive the best cars. They are very conscious of labels." She pursed her wrinkled lips around the filter of her cigarette and sucked the last bit of smoke out of it before dropping the butt into the ash tray to burn out. "Never make a social faux pas. Always be the most courteous and the most prompt. Always send flowers after a business meeting."

Sarah tilted her head. "I should send flowers to men?"

"Oh, yes, *chere!* Yes. The Russians love flowers. Especially the men. The bigger the bouquet the better. It makes them feel very important." She ran her hand up Jason's thigh. "It strokes their ego."

Jason rolled his eyes at Sarah.

Giselle crossed her hands on her knee. "Their *faux pas* will be your power and yours will be theirs. Be careful. You are a beautiful woman and they always have lots of idiots around. While your hosts may be perfectly gracious, watch their bodyguards. They will do plenty of offensive things. The key is to catch them. They will embarrass themselves and your host and that will give you the upper hand in the next negotiation. Listen when they whisper."

Sarah began to realize just how careful she would have to be. She had to listen to everything that was said, never say anything wrong and look fantastic while she did it.

Piece of cake.

Giselle continued. "Always give and demand respect, never lose your temper. And always, always be gracious."

"Okay." Sarah remembered the grace with which she'd conducted herself on Hassan's yacht even though she knew full well what those men were saying behind her back and sometimes right in front of her face. "I can do that." She nodded. "So what exactly is our business, Giselle? How do we play in the big picture?"

The old woman smiled. "They own the poppy fields in Afghanistan. If they don't own them, they pay off the warlords who do. They have the product processed and own the product. We pay off the right people so we can use the roads through Iran, Iraq and Syria unmolested. They use their trucks to transport through to the coast of Syria. Then we use our boats to transport to the ship in Tangiers. Our ship transports the product to Europe and the United States."

"So we handle all the movement of their goods?"

"Yes, for a very large percentage. Without us, they would be standing in Afghanistan with their *boules* in their hands."

"So without us they'd have a stockpile of opium in Afghanistan and no way to get it out? There is no competition for our services?"

Giselle smiled with cigarette-stained teeth. "Exactly."

"Is anyone close to competing with us?"

The old woman nodded. "There was Viktor. He had an air transport service that was competitive. Unfortunately he recently met with an occupational hazard so the business is in flux right now."

Sarah recalled Viktor. He had been the target of their last mission. He had been a great looking guy who had made an unfortunate career choice. He was responsible for her first gunshot wound and the small scar on her shoulder. "Isn't there anyone to take over his routes?"

"Even if his second in command takes over, he's in the Ivanov Organization which has been at war with the Mikhailovich for months now. They won't do business together. We're the only game in town."

Sarah sensed some politics she should be aware of. "What is the Mikhailovich?"

"The Mikhailovich Organization is the Russian family we do business with."

"A family? This seems like a pretty big operation for a family."

"Don't be naive. A criminal family."

"The Russian Mafia?"

"Of course. They run everything in the former Soviet states."

Sarah saw red flags waving all over this situation. They'd had too many botched jobs with Nikolai. There was the incident in Vegas, Viktor, and Vince's kidnapping. Chris had suspected all along that it was red mafia. Now they had confirmation.

What if Nikolai is in the Mikhailovich Organization? What if I have to try to do business with him? He's got a contract out on me.

Sarah turned to Jason. "We've should get Chris on this."

It could get dangerous and ugly fast.

~~~

Jason rolled up to the curb at the airport terminal and immediately ID'd' his target.

Yeah, he's got the look.

Jay Stanstead stood about an inch short of six feet. His hair was about as long as his five o clock shadow. And he was surveying the scene discreetly like a seasoned professional when Jason pulled up in front of him.

Jason stepped out of the Range Rover and walked around the back. He offered a handshake. "Stanstead?"

Stanstead looked him over, nodded and returned the handshake.

"I'm Jason."

"Nice to meet you."

Firm handshake. Good.

Jason took the man's bags and placed them in the back of the truck while Stanstead climbed in the passenger seat.

A few more minutes and they were out of the terminal area. Stanstead spoke first. "So are you the guy I'm relieving?"

"Nah. I'm muscle and odd jobs." Jason took a glance at the man's profile.

Looks the part. Good suit. Sarah will like that. Omega watch. Will'll like that. Looks like a hard man. That'll come in handy.

Curiosity was killing Jason. "So what's your background?"

Stanstead turned a stern glance at Jason. "Sorry, mate. I really can't discuss that. You understand?"

Rather than be offended, Jason was impressed and nodded. "Fair enough."

Damn. This guy will make a great bodyguard.

Jason stifled a grin and drove the rest of the way in satisfied silence.

~~~

Brian shouted down the stairway to the lounge. "Hey, Sarah, Jason just pulled up. They're on their way over now."

Sarah set her Russian Forbes magazine down on the coffee table and walked up to the bridge where Brian watched Jason and the bodyguard through a set of binoculars.

Brian handed her the binoculars. "Go ahead. You know you want to check him out."

Sarah took the binoculars and focused in on the guy walking with Jason. She caught her breath. She couldn't stop herself. "Sweet Jesus. He's hot."

Brian chuckled. "Yeah, I think I've even got a little man crush on him myself."

Sarah focused the binoculars and watched the two men walk down the long dock toward the yacht.

Brock did not disappoint.

The new guy was wearing a tailored, dark suit.

Looks like silk. He's got style.

His hair and his beard were about the same length, about four days growth but very neat. He took sure and steady steps but there was something almost catlike about him. His movements were fluid. He walked like a man who knew he was powerful.

Sexy.

He didn't speak to Jason at all which was interesting since Jason was a real Chatty Cathy most of the time and appeared to be chatting all the way down the dock.

Sarah handed Brian the binoculars and gave him a sideways glance.

Brian threw her a wink. "Let's go see which one of us he likes best."

Sarah gave a mock scowl. "Okay, but if it's you he's fired."

Brian slapped her hand in a semi handshake. "Deal." He went downstairs to the main salon first and Sarah followed a few steps behind.

Jason ushered the new guy into the main salon of the yacht.

A fluttering started inside Sarah's stomach, but she didn't wait for an introduction. She reached out her hand to the new guy. "Hi, I'm Scuro. Thank you for getting here so quickly."

His voice was soft but rugged and laced with an English accent. It was an intriguing combination. "Jay Stanstead. It's a pleasure to meet you, Miss Scuro." He had a warm, firm handshake that sent waves of excitement through her body. Everything about him was captivating.

Sarah smiled and looked into his eyes. She felt instantly at ease with this man, as though they'd known each other forever. "Please, call me Sarah."

"All right, Sarah." There was just a hint of a smile at the outer edges of his eyes. They were a golden hazel color, almost feline.

Sarah realized she was still holding his hand and pulled away embarrassed. "You've met Jason. These guys are Brian, Chris, Will and Vince. My staff." Sarah just couldn't get used to referring to Rig as Vince but it was the only way to set the trap. She watched as Jay shook hands with each man, greeting them by name. All the while, Jason stood back and smiled like a little kid at Christmas.

What the hell is going on with him?

Sarah touched Will's shoulder. "Will, would you please get Jay a drink?"

She smiled at Jay. She couldn't help smiling at him and that annoyed her. She'd seen attractive men before so why should she turn into a pussycat for this one? "Would you excuse us for a moment? Have a seat and make yourself comfortable. You aren't on the clock yet and Will has some good Scotch and cigars if you like that sort of thing."

She could sense him watching her and heat flushed her cheeks as she led Jason out onto the deck and closed the door behind them. "What the hell are you grinning like a little girl for?"

Jason laughed. "Was I?" He almost sounded giddy.

"Uh, yeah!"

His eyes opened wide like they always did when he was excited about something. Sarah usually saw that look when he went shopping for guns or motorcycles.

"I've got a good feeling about this guy, Sarah. A really good feeling."

"Why? Did you swap war stories between here and the airport?"

Jason leaned on the deck rail. "No, that's the funny part." He shrugged. "I don't know what it is. He just seems like the real deal, a no-bullshit, just do it kind of guy, like us."

"Okay. That's good to know." Sarah shook her head. "Brian's already got a man crush on him. Let's go see if he's bewitched Will and Chris too."

Jason opened the door and held it as she walked back into the salon.

She was pleased to see Jay sitting with the rest of the guys, talking and laughing like old friends. He and Will were smoking cigars. Chris, Brian and Rig were drinking beer and chuckling away about something that had apparently been quite funny.

Jay's gaze met hers as she entered the room and he stood.

Oh my God, he stood when I walked into the room!

Heat positively burned her cheeks this time. "Please, sit down. They're treating you well?"

"Yes, very well. Thanks."

Her physical reaction to him and feeling like a giddy, nervous schoolgirl around him annoyed the hell out of her. "I have to make a few phone calls so please carry on. I'll be done in a few minutes."

She moved to one of the overstuffed chairs in the corner and lit a cigarette before calling Giselle to confirm her first trip to Moscow. Then she called the pilot with the details while she listened to Jay and the guys swap war stories. His voice both calmed and excited her. Maybe it was the familiarity and easy lilt of the accent but Sarah didn't think so. It was something else. Every few minutes she caught him watching her. She warmed inside and couldn't help but smile at him.

What is it about this guy that makes him win everyone over almost instantly?

Sarah sat back and watched the magic that was Jay Stanstead. For the first time in a long time, she stopped thinking about Vince.

Seven

Morocco

Sarah woke with a start to a noise from the balcony. Adrenaline popped through her veins bringing her from sleep to fully alert within seconds. She grabbed her knife from under the pillow and sat upright. She listened for a moment and realized it was the sound of china and silver.

If someone was trying to break in they sure as hell wouldn't stop for coffee.

She put the knife in the nightstand drawer, ran a brush through her hair, slipped on a short robe and walked over to the French doors opening them to find Jay sitting at the table.

He looked the perfect businessman, blue dress pants, a starched white shirt, and a stunning red silk tie.

I remember admiring that one in the Hermes shop in Vegas. This guy has great taste.

Gold cufflinks sparkled in the morning sun. He peered over the paper he'd been reading, the picture of all things civilized. He smiled. "Good morning." He set the paper on the table. "I hope you don't mind. It was too nice a day to take my breakfast inside." He stood and pulled out a chair for her. "Will you join me?"

Sarah was suddenly very aware she was wearing a robe, just a robe and nothing but a robe. "I think I'm a little under dressed."

"Don't be silly. It's just coffee, not dinner and a movie." His eyes sparkled. "Suit yourself. I already checked the area. Nothing out here but me and open sea."

Sarah smiled and sat. " That's reassuring."

Jay picked up the coffee pot and poured a cup. "How do you like it?"

"Just black, thank you. You don't have to serve me. You're my bodyguard, not my butler."

He handed her a full coffee cup. "I consider the courtesy fair trade for good company."

"I hope I won't disappoint you." Sarah took a cautious sip.

"Somehow I don't think you could." Jay took a drink of his own coffee without taking his gaze off her.

Sarah was unaccustomed to blushing but this guy had her doing it like a schoolgirl. A twinge of guilt rippled through her. She was enjoying this man's company and she had no idea where in the world Vince might be, or if he was alive.

Moscow

Vince climbed the stairs to Angelica's apartment on the fourth floor, knocked on the door and waited.

Angelica opened her door and smiled at him.

Did she sleep in her over sprayed hair and makeup?

He gathered from her wardrobe that she knew how to shop and an introduction by a local could be helpful. "Excuse me for bothering you but would you know a good store where I could buy some new clothes?"

"By yourself?"

"Yes, unless you'd like to accompany me and give me a woman's opinion?"

"Shopping?" Her eyes lit and she opened the door wider and waved him in. "We can't have you walking around town in jeans the entire time you're here. I should help you. Let me get my coat." She reached into the closet and grabbed a heavy wool garment.

"Am I interrupting your plans? You look like you were about to go somewhere." Vince took the coat from her and held it as she slipped into it.

"No, no. I was just reading." She turned toward him and smiled. "Thank you."

He offered her his arm. "Shall we?"

She took his arm and they walked downstairs and left the building.

Angelica led him to a shop several blocks away.

They entered and a man with a glowing smile came from behind the counter reaching for Angelica's hands. "Ah, Linka! How wonderful to see you."

Angelica greeted him with a regal smile. "Thank you, Boris. It is lovely to see you again."

"What can I do for you today?" Boris hurried to help her with her coat.

"My new friend, Vincent, has just moved into my building and needs to shop for some clothes. I thought perhaps you could help him."

The man smiled again and shook Vince's hand. "Of course. Of course. But first, Linka, please sit down." He directed her to a chair and motioned to the boy behind the counter. "Peter, please bring Miss Leonova some hot tea."

Boris hung her heavy coat on a rack behind the chair. "Sir?" He took Vince's jacket and hung it up as well.

"Thank you."

Peter arrived with Angelica's tea and disappeared.

"Casual or dress clothes? What can I help the gentleman with today?" Boris rubbed his hands together and looked at Vince.

"A little of both. I packed light and only brought jeans and a few shirts. I'll be here for at least a few months and need enough of everything so as not to look like a bum."

Boris shrugged. "The jeans are much more common these days, but a man of your stature would be even more impressive in something just a bit more businesslike. May I suggest some long trousers, button-down shirts and perhaps some shoes?"

Vince nodded and spread his hands, palm up. "I place myself in your capable hands."

Boris' cheeks rose in a polite smile. "It is not important for clothes to have designer labels, but do you have a preference?"

Vince slid his hands into his pockets and rocked slightly on his toes. "Boris, you know the lady I am escorting today better than I do. Do you think we should throw a few designers in just for good measure? We can't have her being seen with a slob."

Angelika looked on with a serene smile while Boris sold Vince an entire wardrobe.

The expensive purchase was a necessary expense and would pay off well in goodwill and street cred. Boris added the purchases up on a small notepad. Vince pulled out his wallet and counted out cash for the man.

"We will do the alterations now and Peter will deliver everything to you this afternoon."

"Thank you, Boris." Vince reached to shake his hand. "It was a pleasure meeting you. You've been a great help."

"It was my pleasure, sir. Boris nodded. Any friend of Linka's is always welcome."

Vince walked over to Angelika and helped her with her coat.

Angelika nodded at the shopkeeper. "Goodbye, Boris."

"Goodbye, Linka. Thank you and come again soon for a visit."

Vince held the door for Angelika.

Outside the shop she took his arm again.

He smiled down at the little woman who held herself as though she were a queen gracing her subjects with a visit. "Is it too early for lunch?"

"Of course not." She patted his arm. "Don't you know it is always lunchtime for old women?"

"Old is a state of mind. Lead the way, Miss Leonova."

Angelika took him to a small cafe about a block away.

Just as in the clothing store, the proprietor fell over himself trying to make her comfortable.

Vince enjoyed sitting back and watching the show. The owner knew all of Linka's favorites and, although none of them appeared on the menu, they were all delivered promptly without a single order being taken. He envied her the familiarity of her neighbors.

I wish I had a neighborhood. I've been on the move so long nothing feels like home.

After hours of conversation and good food, interrupted by well-wishers, busybodies, and Linka's adoring public, Vince understood that Linka really was something of a queen in this neighborhood.

Being seen with her obviously won't hurt my reputation any.

He paid for the meal and left a healthy tip for the service.

The air was almost warm with the midday winter sun when they stepped outside the restaurant. Vince looked down at the old woman. "That was a great meal. Would you like to go home now or should we take advantage of the weather and have a little walk?"

She patted his arm. "How nice of you to ask. It is a lovely day for a stroll."

Vince was amazed at the old woman's energy. They walked most of the afternoon though Linka wore high heels and the sidewalks were icy.

She showed him around the neighborhood, pointing out each grocery, deli and liquor store he should shop at, even going so far as to make introductions to shopkeepers, her friends and acquaintances along the way.

Vince laughed to himself at the simplicity of it all.

This woman was either a shrewd judge of character or a fool to be introducing him to everyone the way she did. He hoped it was the former.

Morocco

Sarah sat on the couch in Giselle's sitting area and tried not to stare at Jay as he drank his tea.

Giselle had given Sarah her last briefing and was now dialing to set the wheels in motion for Sarah's first business trip to Moscow. She began with small talk but quickly got down to business.

"No, no, Anatole. I simply cannot travel as much anymore. I am getting older. It is time for me to think about retiring and spending my days in bed with lovers instead of working. I am sending my associate, Scuro, for this meeting on Thursday. I expect you to show the same respect to my associate that you would show me."

She listened and then nodded. "Yes, yes. Scuro will be taking over the whole operation." She paused. "Oh, very capable. I'm sure you'll be impressed." She nodded again. "Yes, Scuro will be there on Thursday."

Giselle grinned across the room at Sarah as she hung up. "With any luck they'll assume Scuro is a man. That's the only freebie you'll get in this business, ma chere. Use it."

Moscow

Vince heard a racket in the hallway downstairs and tried to tune it out and concentrate on the evening news. He heard a man's voice and what sounded like at least two women.

Domestic issues.

He clicked the remote to mute the volume on the television.

The hair on the back of his neck stood up.

Wait! That's the old lady's voice.

Every nerve tensed for action. He yanked on his shirt, not bothering to button it and ran down the two flights of stairs, three steps at a time. He arrived at the bottom landing just in time to see a young woman with a bloody face screaming and a man throwing the old landlady to the floor.

There was no time to stop and think… He jumped into the fray instinctively. He lunged forward and hit the stranger so hard the guy bounced off the wall behind him and fell unconscious to the floor.

When Vince turned to check on the old woman, the bloody girl was already by her side. "I'm so sorry. I'm so sorry I brought him here. Please forgive me, Linka?"

The old woman sat up slowly with Vince's help.

He reached an arm around and under her shoulders to keep her steady. "Are you all right?"

"Yes, yes. I am fine. Just a little bruise or two." She looked into his eyes. "Help me inside Svetlana's apartment where I can catch my breath, Vika."

Vince smiled at her use of the familiar form of his name in Russian and lifted her to her feet.

I rate a nickname. That's progress.

Svetlana ran inside her apartment to fluff pillows on a tiny chair for Angelica. "I'm so sorry. I'm so sorry for the trouble. I'll make some tea."

When Angelica had settled into the chair, Vince nodded at the unconscious man in the hallway. "What would you like done with him?"

Angelica's eyes narrowed. "Put him outside in the snow, with the rest of the trash."

Vince grinned. "Yes, ma'am."

The old woman has guts and style.

He hefted the unconscious man over his shoulder and carried him outside, dumping him on the snow bank in front of the building.

This could be really good or really bad, but that fucker had a beat down coming.

He discreetly checked the man's chest for the telltale tattooed cross of the *vor y zakone*, the Russian Mafia.

Bless the saints. No vor here.

He walked back into the building, closing the exterior door as he did. The door to Svetlana's first floor apartment still stood open. He peeked in to see Angelica apparently comfortable and drinking a cup of tea.

Svetlana, her face still bloody from the beating she took, ushered Vince in. "Thank you so much. I'm so sorry. I'm Svetlana. Please come and sit with Linka while I clean up."

"Of course." Vince sat in a small chair near Angelica.

Svetlana was a petite brunette with a beautiful body. She moved quickly for someone who had clearly taken a beating. She placed a cup of warm tea in his hands and disappeared into the bathroom. Vince wondered what she would look like under all that blood.

"How are you Angelica Leonova? Do you need a doctor? Should we call the police?"

She glowed with a sublime smile and covered his hand with hers. "You must call me Linka, my friend. You are a good man to protect two helpless women the way you did."

Vince shrugged. "Any man would have done the same."

She shook her head. "No. Not any man, only a good one." She pointed to his chest.

He had yet to button his shirt when he came back in from outside.

"No tattoos. You are not *Vor?*" She raised a brow and grinned. "You are not as bad as you would have me think." She watched as Vince buttoned his shirt. "Misha will visit me tonight. I will tell him about this man that was here and he will want to meet you. Come to my apartment at eight. You will have dinner with us."

He demurred so as not to seem over eager. "Oh, no. I couldn't impose." Vince shook his head.

She laughed, her eyes sparkling. Her laugh was like butterflies filling the room. She leaned forward and touched his chin like a mother might. "Oh, no, you misunderstand. That was not a question for you to answer. It was a statement. Now go shave and I will see you promptly at eight."

Vince grinned, impressed with the old woman's spunk, and set his tea on the table and stood. "Yes, ma'am."

~~~

Vince took one last look at the bouquet of flowers in his hand to be sure none of the blooms were wilting and knocked on the door of Linka's fourth floor apartment.

Linka opened the door almost instantly. "There he is and right on time." She smiled and accepted the flowers Vince handed her as she ushered him inside.

An elderly man sat on her sofa. He had a medium build but held his chin high. He looked like he had once been a very powerful man. A cane stood nearby.

"Misha, this is the young man I told you about. Mikhail Andreovich Drugov, this is my new friend and protector Vincent."

Vince walked to the sofa and shook the man's hand. "It is a pleasure to meet you, sir." He meant it. This was the godfather of Moscow's mafia.

Misha's handshake was firm and strong. "The pleasure is mine. I want to thank you for taking care of my Linka today." He motioned for Vince to sit in the chair across from him.

"No thanks are necessary, Sir." Vince sat and looked the man over carefully. The old man's hands were liberally tattooed and he was particularly well dressed. The real deal. Old school *Vor*. He's probably covered with prison tattoos to prove it.

Misha seemed to be taking a visual inventory of his own. "You are not a Muscovite. Where are you from?"

"I'm American but I would prefer to keep that information between us, sir."

The old man's eyes narrowed. "Are you an American spy?"

Vince looked the man in the eyes. "No, sir."

"Then what brings you to Moscow?"

"Personal business. I'm here to settle a debt."

The old man nodded. "That is a most dangerous business."

The old man's response and the careful way he said it conveyed to Vince this man understood the very personal business of murder. "It can be. Yes, sir."

~~~

When the last of the dishes had been cleared from the table and Linka had served coffee and pastries for dessert, she turned to Misha. "I'm thinking of buying a car."

Misha took a sip of his coffee. "Why would you need a car?"

"I am getting older and the winters seem to be colder. A walk to the market can be quite a task on a cold day." She glanced at Vince.

The old man took another sip. "Just call me. I will have a driver take you."

She shook her head. "No, I think it is time I should have a car of my own."

Misha nodded. "I'll take care of it."

Vince drank his coffee quietly. Yes, this was a man who was used to taking care of things.

~~~

Vince rolled over in bed and checked the time. It was still early.

Three sets of heavy footsteps walked past his apartment.

More trouble?

He jumped out of bed and opened his door to look up the stairs toward Linka's apartment. A tall, dark haired man with a well-trimmed beard and light blue eyes looked down at him.

"You're Vincent, right? Misha mentioned you." He smiled and his blue eyes sparkled. He seemed amused. "No need to worry. Misha asked us to bring some cars by for Linka to see."

Vince nodded and closed his door.

~~~

Vince hadn't expected a visit from Misha but here the man was drinking coffee in Vince's room.

Misha took a sip from a tiny china cup and nodded. "My man told me you seemed alarmed when they came to show Linka some cars. I appreciate your attention to her safety. She tells me you do not have a job. Is that true?"

"Yes, it is."

"I should introduce you to my son. Perhaps he will have something you can do. Do you have any skills?"

Vince knew full well that Misha's son was The Mikhailovich, the man that ran Moscow's mob. "Thank you very much, but I am not looking for a job."

I don't need an undercover gig, I just want to kill Nikolai Federov and be on my way.

The old man eyed Vince. "No man is so rich that he can afford to turn down friends, Vincent. You seem like a smart young man. I should not have to explain that it often benefits a man to have well placed friends here in Moscow. What I am offering you is an introduction to some people who could be very good friends."

Vince smiled and nodded.

He's right. It couldn't hurt to have these guys watching my six. This is my ticket in.

"Of course, I would appreciate meeting your son or any friends you see fit to introduce me to."

The old man placed his tattooed hands, one on top of the other, on the brass head of his cane. "They are not so much my friends as they are my family, Vika."

A good sign. He's using the familiar form of my name.

"I understand, sir. You're very generous. Thank you."

The old man stood. "Expect somebody to come by tomorrow afternoon."

Vince nodded. "I look forward to it, sir."

Eight

Morocco

Sarah walked into the sitting room that she shared with Jay. She caught the faint scent of his after shave and took a slow deep breath.

So good.

Jay looked up at her and smiled. He folded his newspaper and set it down on the table beside his chair before standing. "Good morning."

"Good morning. I hope I'm not interrupting your reading."

"Not at all. I like to stay on top of the dailies wherever I am. It helps me be prepared for the job. Nothing here but yacht parties and art exhibits." He motioned to a chair. "Have a seat."

She slipped into the chair across from him and laced her fingers together. Her thumbs seemed to involuntarily fidget behind her fingers as she searched her mind for a way to bring up what she thought would surely be a difficult subject.

"Jay, we need to talk about this trip to Moscow."

He leaned forward, elbows on his knees, and looked her in the eyes, giving her his full attention.

Nervous butterflies fluttered inside her. "These guys I'll be doing business with in Moscow are throwbacks from a much more chauvinist era."

He nodded. "They're gangsters, right?"

Sarah took a deep breath. "In a word, yes. The thing is, I'm going into this with a bit of a handicap."

He tilted his head slightly. "How so?"

"Being female."

His lips curled into a faint smile. "That you are." He continued to focus on her.

" They have a certain stereotype of businesswomen there."

"Sarah, I know that. Let's stop beating about the bush. What do you need from me? How can I help you do what needs to be done?"

Sarah smiled, suddenly nervous as she crossed and uncrossed her legs, then grimaced. She hated feeling so vulnerable with a man who was supposed to be an employee.

Oh, for Pete's sake, buck up, Stevens!

"Here's the thing."

Jay smiled and his eyes creased with silent laughter. "Yes, let's get to the thing, Sarah."

"If I go in hard as nails they'll assume I'm a dyke and I'll have even less credibility."

"Okay." He made a rolling motion with his hands. "Still waiting for *the thing*."

"By the same token, if they think I have a lover and I'm tough in business, I'll gain credibility."

Jay nodded, still listening.

She took another deep breath. "I know it isn't in your job description and I have no right to ask..."

A smile spread across Jay's face and his eyes did that sparkly thing again. He leaned back in his chair, clearly amused at how awkward Sarah felt.

"All right, would it be too much to ask you to pretend to be my lover?" Sarah grimaced as heat made another rush toward her cheeks. "You don't have to actually *be* my lover, just let them think you are." She shifted in her seat.

What the hell is it about this guy that makes me so fricking nervous?

"What? Are you kidding me? That's more like a Christmas bonus." He loosened his silk tie. "Jay Stanstead never does anything halfway. If you need a lover, I'm your man." He started unbuttoning his shirt. What say we start now and get a little practice in?"

Shock left her speechless. She gazed over his solid, hairy chest and rumble strip abs. Sweat broke out on her forehead and she gripped her hands into tight fists by her sides so he might not notice they were shaking.

"Uh...as tempting as all that is," she motioned with her hand at the picture of virility in front of her, "I think we'll do just fine without the practice."

Jay shrugged. "Practice makes perfect."

"No, I think we're good. Thanks for...uh...understanding."
Sarah stood.

I've got to get out of here before I take him up on that.

"All right then." He began buttoning his shirt, never taking his sparkling gaze off her. "If you change your mind, I'm here for you twenty-four-seven."

God help me.

"Thanks. I appreciate it." She headed for the door and bolted toward her room.

"Really. I'll be right here."

She spoke over her shoulder without turning around. "Thank you, Jay."

"Ready to practice."

Sarah closed the door behind her and leaned against it to stop herself from going back into the sitting room. Her blood coursed through her veins like a freight train. All she could hear was her heart beating.

My God. He's not only charming as hell and funny, he's Goddamned gorgeous.

~~~

Sarah slipped her Rolex on her wrist as she strolled into the sitting room, steeled against Jay's overwhelming charisma. When she told Brock she wanted a guy who was up on world events, she had no idea he'd find one who was so completely up to the minute. "Jay, please don't take offense, you're always dressed very well but we need to really wow these Russians. Do you mind if I take a look at your wardrobe so we can see if we need to buy anything before we go?"

Jay looked up from his paper and grinned wide. "You want to check my knickers and see what I'm packing?"

Hell, yeah, I want to see what you're packing.

She smiled and paused just long enough to make him think she was considering his offer. "If you don't mind."

He stood and adjusted his tie before leading her into his bedroom adjoining the sitting room. "Allow me to show you my closet."

71

The walk-in was large by most standards but standing next to Jay made it feel very small.

This guy is good.

Everything was hung carefully spaced two inches apart. Two suits, three pairs of dress slacks, six white shirts and ties. There must have been a dozen ties. All silk. All exquisite.

Sarah reached for one that matched the color of Jay's eyes and fondled the fine silk between her fingers. "You have excellent taste."

Jay reached for the tie and their hands touched for just a moment. "Do you like it?"

A jolt shot through her body and she turned to find herself face to face with Jay. "I do."

Jay's gaze didn't leave Sarah's.

She should look away but she didn't want to. Sure, she should be focusing on just work and not falling into another situation where romance complicated work, but he was too attractive to avoid.

He flipped his collar up and whipped off the tie he wore.

I shouldn't do this, but I'm going to.

Sarah reached up to loop the other tie around his neck. It was a great excuse to touch him. To touch the smooth silk of the tie, the crisp cotton of his shirt and him, especially him. She straightened his collar and grazed his neck with her fingers.

Just don't fall again. Don't be distracted from the job.

Jay's voice startled her from her thoughts. "Who is he?"

Her fingers fumbled with the tie. "Excuse me?"

That rock is hard to miss. Who wouldn't ask?

"The guy who gave you that ring. I haven't seen you with anyone but your staff. Is he here?"

Looking into Jay's eyes, Sarah struggled for a response. "I shouldn't wear it but it is beautiful. I never had a diamond before." She shrugged. "Would you believe it's complicated?"

She focused on the tie.

He reached up and held her left hand in his. "Complicated? Are you together or not?" His voice seemed to go down an octave and her breasts became very sensitive against her lace bra.

"Not."

"Then it isn't as complicated as all that, is it?"

The closet seemed even smaller than it had a moment before. She took a deep breath and then another to no avail.

She let her hands drop and turned away. "You'd better tie that tie. We'll make a stopover in Milan on our way to Moscow and pick up a few more things for you. I have some phone calls to make." Without waiting for a response she hurried from the closet and went directly to her room.

My God, what's happening? Am I rebounding? He's my bodyguard, not some gigolo!

Milan

Sarah gazed out the window of the limo as they pulled up to the boutique. Milan was beautiful at night and she loved the special treatment high-end boutiques provided on her Agency expense account. Jay stepped out of the limousine first. He straightened his jacket and then extended his hand for Sarah. He leaned close as she stood and whispered in her ear. "We should probably get started on that pretend lovers thing now, eh?"

Butterflies fluttered in her stomach. "I suppose so." She took his hand and stepped carefully out of the limo.

Waiting for her on the sidewalk was an impeccably dressed young man. He smiled. "Miss Stevens?"

She flashed her most charming smile. "Yes, and this is Mr. Stanstead. I trust you're ready for us?"

"Yes, please come inside." He led Sarah and Jay into a luxurious boutique. "Your assistant said that time was an issue, Miss Stevens."

"Yes, we need to fly to Moscow tomorrow. That won't be a problem, will it?"

"Of course not. We have the items for you in the sizes you requested and we have a tailor who will do Mr. Stanstead's alterations tonight. We'll deliver them all to your hotel first thing in the morning."

"Perfect."

~~~

Sarah sipped her wine while the stylist helped Jay.

If Macy's added a comfortable chair and a glass of wine like this place did, I'll bet they'd have happier customers.

They had chosen a complete designer wardrobe for him and were fitting the formalwear now.

He strolled out of the dressing room wearing a tuxedo that looked like it was made just for him.

"I love the cut of that tux."

The stylist seemed impressed. "Yes, he wears it well, doesn't he?"

"He certainly does." Sarah crossed her legs as warmth spread between them. "How do you like it, Jay?"

A smile curled his lips as he tugged at the cuffs and looked into the mirror. "Whatever makes you happy, pet."

"We'll take it, along with three shirts. A man who looks that good is bound to get lipstick on a collar or two."

Did I just say that out loud?

Jay gave Sarah a sideways glance. He didn't seem bothered by the comment and she thought she noticed the edges of his lips turn up in a discreet smile.

"He'll need an overcoat, something warm for Moscow weather, and scarves too." Sarah couldn't take her gaze off him.

He's a good looking man. I can appreciate beauty. It doesn't mean I want to hop in the sack with him. And now I'm lying to myself!

Sarah began to wonder if being horny had something to do with the job. Was she becoming a female Brian?

"Do you prefer a three button or a double breasted coat?"

"I'm partial to double breasted. What do you like, Jay?"

Jay looked up at the stylist. "The lady is partial to double breasted so double breasted it shall be."

Sarah took another sip of her Shiraz and stole a glance at Jay as he removed the tuxedo coat and slung it over his shoulder before returning to the dressing room. She allowed herself the guilty pleasure of watching him walk away.

I'm not dead yet. There's nothing wrong with appreciating a nice ass when I see one.

Jay stole a glance over his shoulder.

Sarah tried to avert her gaze but she hadn't been fast enough.

"I saw that." He laughed and closed the dressing room door behind him.

The stylist walked into the room with a black wool overcoat over his arm. "If you don't mind me saying so Miss Stevens, you have impeccable taste." He turned toward the dressing room. "How do you enjoy having a woman dress you, Mr. Stanstead?"

Jay spoke from over the dressing room door. "I rather like the undivided attention but think I might like it a bit more if the woman were *un*dressing me. When do we get to do that, pet?"

The stylist grinned at Sarah and picked up his notebook. "I'll just cross sleepwear off the list."

Moscow

Vince tiptoed to the side of the door and peeked quickly through the hole to see who had knocked.

One man.

"Who is it?" He ducked across the doorway, gun drawn, and braced himself on the other side just in case it was a hit man aiming at the sound of his voice.

"Alexander Sergeyevich Avilov. I am a friend of Mikhailovich."

Vince tucked his handgun into the back of his trousers and flipped his shirt tail over it. He opened the door with a friendly smile. "Please come in. I'm Vincent." He reached to shake the man's hand.

Avilov surveyed the room while he removed his black leather gloves and then shook Vince's hand. "You answer the door like a man who is familiar with thugs. Are you a thug?"

Vince answered with honesty. It made for fewer stories to keep straight. "Some might say so."

"And you are Misha's new friend?"

Vince motioned to one of the chairs at the small table. "He and I have met, yes. Would you like to sit?"

"You have more than met. It seems he's quite impressed with you. Misha isn't a man who is easily impressed."

Vince knew he was being checked out. This guy was most likely a captain in the organization. They wouldn't trust an interview about the boss' immediate family to just anyone. "He seems like a very good man. Would you like some coffee?"

Avilov gave a crooked smile. "Thank you."

Moscow

Jay opened the door and escorted Sarah into the plush waiting area attended by a large man in a dark suit.

Sarah stopped inside the door and tossed her hair to shake off the snow.

Jay's hands gently stroked her shoulders as he helped her take off her coat.

She stopped to enjoy the moment. Her body warmed instantly.

Sarah eyed the man behind the desk and addressed him in Russian. "Tell your boss Scuro is here."

The man ignored Sarah and addressed Jay. "Please have a seat, sir."

Jay waited while Sarah sat in one of the chairs, then situated himself in a chair nearby. Sara smiled as she leaned close to whisper in Jay's ear. "This is good. He'll be embarrassed and I'll be one up. Go with it." She paused there a moment to enjoy his aftershave.

The big man opened an office door and spoke to the person inside. "Scuro is here."

The response was amusing. "And waiting? Don't keep him waiting!"

The big man spoke only to Jay. "You may go in sir."

Sarah moved to walk into the office but the man blocked the door.

"You can wait out here, miss."

"I'll be just a moment, pet." Jay straightened his Armani jacket and walked into the office, closing the door behind him.

Sarah sat in a nearby chair and crossed her legs. Amusement and satisfaction bubbled together inside her. She lit a cigarette and smiled at the guard.

A second later Anatole dashed out of the office. "Idiot!" He extended his hand as he hurried to Sarah. "Miss Scuro, I'm so very sorry for the mix-up."

Sarah stood, straightened her skirt and tossed her hair over her right shoulder, pointedly ignoring his hand. Satisfied that he was properly embarrassed at the mix-up she gave the guard a quick brow lift and a nod. He and Anatole were visibly mortified.

She ran a hand over Jay's shoulder, inhaling the light scent of aftershave. The silk suit felt delicious under her fingertips. "Jay, you can keep that young man company. Perhaps he could find us some coffee?" She looked back at the guard who nodded obediently. "Yes, Miss Scuro."

~~~

Sarah emerged from the office an hour later.

Jay set his coffee down on a nearby table and stood as she entered the waiting room.

I love when he does that.

The guard followed his lead.

Jay helped her into her coat, running his hands down her arms, sending a wave of wanting cascading through her body. He slipped his own coat on without buttoning it, and they exited the building quickly.

Jay started the Mercedes sedan and pulled into traffic before speaking. He glanced at Sarah as he turned a corner. "How did it go?"

She smiled at him. "It went very well. Anatole was mortified at the mix-up and our negotiations reflected that. What did you say to him?"

"I said I hoped he had a good reason for keeping 'The Scuro' out in a waiting room with a dolt of a guard who didn't even have the decency to offer her something warm to drink on a cold day."

Sarah laughed a hearty, throaty laugh. The situation was too funny not to enjoy. "You played it perfectly." She touched his hand on the stick shift. "Well done, Jay. We make a great team."

He turned his hand and held Sarah's for just a moment. "Yeah, we do all right."

Sarah took a deep breath. He was definitely an attractive man but having him hold her hand just for that moment sent her reeling. She swallowed hard and focused on the road ahead.

Nine

Moscow

Heavy footsteps on the stairs outside his apartment distracted Vince from the television news program. He listened carefully and recognized the rhythm. A glance through the peephole confirmed this. Vince opened the door. "Hello, Alexander."

"Misha asked me to show you this photograph." He turned his cellphone toward Vince to show him a picture. "Do you know this man?"

Vince looked at the photo. It was the man who'd beaten the girl downstairs, the guy he'd thrown out with the trash. "Yeah, he's the guy who pushed Linka around and beat the girl downstairs." He stepped back from the door and motioned a welcome. "Please, come in."

Alexander stepped inside as Vince closed the door. "You saw him do this?"

Vince pulled a chair away from the table. "Yes."

"Have you seen him lately?" Alexander slid the phone into his coat pocket but remained standing.

Vince shook his head. "I don't think he'll be coming back here."

"Why not?"

"Because the last time he was here he was knocked unconscious and tossed out in the snow."

"You did that?" He seemed surprised.

"Yes."

Alexander grinned. "Good." He motioned toward the door. "Come with me."

Vince turned off the TV and grabbed his jacket on the way out. He followed Alexander downstairs to where his car had been left with the engine running. They drove in silence to a nearby neighborhood. When Alexander turned onto a side street, Vince noticed a group of three men talking on the sidewalk.

Alexander slammed on the brakes, shut off the car and jumped out.

One of the men broke into a run at the sight of Alexander. Vince jumped out of the car to chase the man he'd last seen unconscious on a snow bank, the man who had pushed Linka around. Cutting through an alley, he came out the other side just in time to tackle the man.

The man struggled but Vince held him down in the snow. "Please, please? I have money."

Alexander pulled a Glock pistol from his belt and pointed it at the man. "Let him stand."

Shit just got real.

Vince steadied himself on one knee and then stood to step away as the man struggled in the icy snow to face Alexander.

The man's simpering voice grated on Vince's nerves like fingernails on a chalkboard. He pleaded with Alexander. "Alexander Sergeyevich Avilov, please. I did not know who she was." The man shook all over and a dark steamy stain traveled from his crotch to the snow below, leaving a yellow stain on the blanket of white.

Alexander appeared disgusted as he spat in the snow, still breathing heavy. "But you do now." Without hesitation, Alexander dispatched the man with a single shot between the eyes.

The man flopped to the ground before Alexander could tuck the gun under his belt.

With a tilt of Alexander's head, he motioned Vince back to the car.

It was a perfect kill shot. The poor bastard dropped like a wet rag, his brains a red Rorschach on the white snow behind him. Vince wondered in silence what kind of woman rated a hit for a slap around as they drove back to Vince's apartment. Clearly Linka was more than just a family friend of the local vor.

When Alexander pulled up to the building he leveled his gaze at Vince. "This stays between us."

Vince shrugged. "Of course." Vince opened the door and stepped out of the car.

Alexander drove away into the grey winter day before Vince made it to the front steps.

~~~

Vince had just shut off the late night news when his door was nearly knocked off its hinges. "Police, open the door!"

Vince bit his lower lip. *I'm either taking the fall or getting tested.* He hopped out of bed and into his pants, tucking his Sig into the breadbox on the counter by the door. He opened the door to see two of Moscow's finest. They didn't look happy.

"May I help you?"

They each grabbed one of Vince's arms. "Come with us." They dragged him roughly down the stairs and shoved him into the back seat of a police car that had been waiting in front of the building. When they arrived at the nearby police station, they pulled him out of the vehicle and tried to trip him as they pulled him up the icy steps. This wasn't the first time Vince had been captured and roughed up. He was too surefooted and this seemed to aggravate them because their grips became tighter and they swung him into the door frame on the way in the building. Once inside, they pulled him through a hallway to a small windowless interrogation room.

~~~

Vince examined the Moscow Police interrogation room he was in from his handcuffed position on an old metal chair in the center.

Great. I'm here on a tourist visa with no cover, no job and no connections. I'm about to either get deported or get a shakedown.

"Do you know this man?" The heavy cop who was questioning him handed him a photo of the man he'd just seen Alexander kill.

Vince nodded. "He was in my building, beating a girl a few days ago."

"Did you kill this man?"

"No."

"Do you know who did?"

"No."

"What do you know about Mikhailovich?"

"Nothing."

The fat cop looked at himself in the two way mirror. Interrogation rooms only had mirrors when they were two-way and by the looks of these guys' hair, they rarely used a mirror at all. "He's lying. Lock him up until he talks."

~~~

After three days of cabbage soup, weak interrogation and a small beating that couldn't stand up to the punch he'd received when Sarah Stevens thought he had been playing her back in Las Vegas, Vince stepped outside the Moscow police station feeling surprisingly rested. The only things on his mind were a hot shower, a change of clothes, and a good steak.

Amateurs.

Alexander leaned against his Mercedes sedan, parked across the street, grinning from ear to ear.

"I thought you might like a ride home."

Three days in captivity and a few punches apparently scored me some points.

Vince rubbed his bearded jaw. "Thanks." He opened the passenger door and flopped into the car.

Alexander slipped into the driver's seat and pulled away from the curb. "Three days and you said nothing. I suppose I should thank you."

Vince shrugged. "There was nothing to say."

He looked at Vince's black eye. "How was your treatment?"

"I've had worse from women."

"I have an errand to run. You don't mind coming with me?"

"Not if you don't mind my stench. I haven't showered in days."

They rode the rest of the way in silence.

Alexander drove to a pawn shop several blocks away. He motioned to the glove compartment as he parked the car on the street.

Vince opened it to find his Sig. Had Linka let Alexander into his apartment? Had he broken in? He tucked the handgun into his belt.

"This man owes Mikhailovich some money. The loan is past due."

It was odd that Alexander was collecting a debt himself. Probably another test.

Play it like you mean it.

He followed Alexander into the pawn shop and stood by as he approached the shopkeeper. "You have the money?"

Vince caught the slightest sound and listened carefully. The telltale sound of a shell sliding into a shotgun came from behind a door leading to the back of the shop.

Vince pulled his gun and aimed at the source of the sound.

Alexander pulled his own gun on the shopkeeper.

A shadow moved in the crease between the barely opened door and the wall. Vince squeezed off two shots at knee level and heard the sound of a man wailing in pain and hitting the concrete floor at about the same time a shotgun clanked to the floor.

"Now pay the man so you can get your friend to a doctor." Vince's jaw hurt and he needed a shower. He really didn't care for all the nonsense.

"No more. No more!" The shopkeeper nearly tripped over himself to get to the register. He pulled a bank bag from under the counter, banged on the register, emptied the contents of the drawer into the bank bag, and handed it over to Alexander.

Alexander nodded to Vince. "You're handy to have around."

Vince opened the door of the shop. "I try."

They left and drove quickly to Vince's apartment building.

Alexander parked in front.

"You passed."

"Excuse me, Alexander?"

"My friends call me Sasha. You did well. You knew how to catch a guy on the run. You didn't talk to the police even when they held you for three days. You didn't hesitate to cut down that shotgun in the shop." Alexander grinned. "The Mikhailovich organization values loyalty."

" Those were all tests?"

"They were things that needed doing. You made them easier and gave me an opportunity to learn a little bit about you."

"What about the police?"

Sasha smiled. "Russian police earn about six thousand rubles a month." He shrugged. "Nobody wants to live on that and I like to do my part for law enforcement."

Moscow

82

After being in Moscow for two days, Sarah knew it was time to take care of some overdue business. She picked up her phone off the desk and dialed Will. "Where is Vince?"

"Not a good idea, Sarah."

Sarah rolled her eyes upward. She knew Will was more seasoned at this stuff than she was but she wished he'd stop telling her what was or wasn't a good idea. "I'll be careful. I'll have Jay with me."

"He'll be at Rasputin on Zubovsky Bulvar."

She glanced down at the diamond and pursed her lips. There was a tiny tug at a heartstring as she realized she might enjoy diamonds more than pearls after all.

I'm going to miss your sparkle.

"Thanks." She hung up and knocked on the door between her and Jay's adjoining suites. "Jay, we need to go out."

He opened the door and smiled. "Just let me grab my jacket." He snatched his jacket from a nearby chair, slipped it on and then grabbed his overcoat. He pulled his cell phone from one of the pockets and called the valet. Sarah smiled as they waited for the elevator and he spoke in perfect Russian to request their car be brought around.

They drove to the gentleman's club and pulled up at the valet station.

Sarah watched from the passenger seat of the Mercedes sedan as Vince and two other men walked into the gentleman's club.

Jay looked confused. "Doesn't he work for you?"

"That's his brother. Let's go."

"Into a gentlemen's club? In Moscow?" Jay shook his head as he got out of the car and came around to open Sarah's door. "Bloody hell, I have the best boss ever."

"I know." Sarah smiled as she stepped out of the car and they walked up to the club.

Jay held the purple glass door open. She walked into the nightclub and pointed to the first brunette she saw.

"Do me a favor and ask that girl to give him a private dance but have her stay out of the room."

"Pardon?"

"I need to talk to him."

"Ah, right." Jay waved the brunette over and slipped easily into Russian. "How much for a private dance?"

She leaned into Jay and touched his chest. "That depends on how long you want me to dance."

Sarah swallowed hard at the kick of jealousy that hit her.

Jay smiled at Sarah. "What do you think, pet? An hour?"

Why do I like it so much when he calls me pet?

"Thanks, but better make it half an hour."

The girl looked from Jay to Sarah. "Is it for both of you?"

"No, it's for that guy over there." Jay pointed over to Vince. "The bald guy."

The brunette smiled and stuck her double-D breasts out just a little more. "Oh, sure."

"Here's the catch though." Jay pointed to Sarah. "She's going to go in the room with him and you're going to take a little break, right?"

The girl ran her fingers up Jay's tie and purred. "I could dance for you."

Jay brushed her hand off him like brushing away lint. "No, that's all right. Just get him into the room and go take a break."

"Giving them the room will cost more."

"No problem." Jay doubled her initial price and put the bills in her hand. Jay turned her toward Vince and gave her a firm swat on the butt. "Go on, then. There's a good girl."

The brunette walked over to Vince, introduced herself and pointed to Jay and Sarah.

Vince showed no emotion.

Jay nodded to Vince though the stone cold expression on Jay's face didn't change.

The girl led Vince up a flight of stairs to a private room and then walked out.

Sarah followed with Jay behind her.

Jay took a position just outside the door as Sarah walked into the private room. "I'll be here if you need me."

"Thanks, Jay." Sarah walked into the room and sauntered over to Vince.

He scowled. "How did you know I was here?"

"You aren't the only one with secret skills." She stroked his cheek that was now covered with a short beard.

Was that a glimmer in his eyes?

"You shouldn't have come. It's too dangerous, especially here in Moscow."

"It's okay, I have a capable bodyguard. Brock says he broke a guy's jaw to get this job."

"Who wouldn't?"

It was the familiar easy banter they'd always had when they worked together. They'd slipped back into the co-worker zone. She knew they'd never cut it romantically, and suspected he knew too. Sarah hated loose ends and what ifs. If he wasn't going to make it final then she had to be the one to call it.

"We have a half hour. Let's not waste it." He smiled and bent to kiss her.

"No." She stopped his hands as they were about to cup her face. "We can't."

"It's okay. We paid the dancer and your bodyguard is at the door."

She grabbed his nimble hands with hers. "No. We can't. We have to talk. This is important."

Vince's demeanor cooled. "I see the way he looks at you Sarah. I can't compete with a man who is by your side twenty-four hours a day. I'm not blind. He has a thing for you. Are you sleeping with him?"

Sarah's mouth dropped open.

He's been watching me work and he's jealous?

"Vince. Don't be a douche. We aren't dating. He's my bodyguard. He's supposed to watch me. Letting people think we're lovers gives me street cred with the guys I'm doing business with. He's just my cover." A chill came over her and her stomach knotted. She could have lived this life and still loved him, but he couldn't love her if she lived this life. They needed a clean emotional break. She knew he wanted a completely different life than she did. This was inevitable.

Vince gave her a half smile and shook his head. "You can't pay a man to watch you like that. Not like that." He took a deep breath. "Sarah, the only reminder you have of me is my asshole twin. With him around, you'll easily forget why you fell for me in the first place."

Well, look at that. He's going to be the one to make the break after all.

"Sarah, don't wait for me. In this line of work, either one of us could bite it at any moment. Go be happy. We had a good run. Get your happiness where you can and don't worry about how I'm going to feel."

Her snark got the best of her. "Because you don't have any feelings about it?"

"No, that's not what I'm saying." He looked down at his feet and shook his head. "There's no easy way to do this. I just want you to be happy. I want to know you're being taken care of. No matter what happens, I'll always care about you. Maybe we'll have a future if we get out of this business alive, but if we don't, I don't want to think you'll be pining away over me when you've got plenty of options."

How sweet. He's breaking up with me and I don't feel the least bit like crying. Why is that? Oh yeah, now I remember, I came here to break up with him.

Sarah cleared her throat. "Well, I guess that's all that needs to be said." She slipped the ring from her finger and nestled the four carat solitaire in the ring box she'd had in her coat pocket.

Vince sighed. Was he relieved?

She handed him the box. "Was there anything else?"

"You knew?"

"A man in love doesn't end a conversation with 'take care of yourself'. I thought I'd give you a chance to change your mind."

"Are we okay?"

She smiled and kissed his cheek. "Of course."

He lit a cigarette and sat in one of the club chairs. "Okay, so tell me about your bodyguard. Is he tough? Has he got the stones to do this work?"

Note to self. Learn to switch gears quickly.

"He's former British Army, S.A.S. He's tough enough."

"Can he take a punch?"

Sarah thought about the glimpse she'd had of Jay's abs and chest. "Absolutely."

"Is he a good shot?"

"I don't know yet but he's fast on his feet."

"That's handy. Is he a good driver?"

"He was in the S.A.S. Mobility Troop. You can't get much better than that."

"Did Will check him out?"

Oh, come on now!

"Yeah, of course Will checked him out. What do you think, we're incapable of running a proper operation without you? He's highly decorated, highly recommended and in demand. His military records are locked tight. There was a lot of classified stuff that even Chris couldn't get to."

"Good. I know you get a wild hair every once in a while and might think about ditching him but don't. Keep him close. He looks like a real pro."

"I have no intention of ditching him."

There was a knock at the door and Jay poked his head in with an apologetic nod. "Sarah, we need to get going. The manager is getting his knickers in a twist."

Vince looked at Sarah with the soft brown gaze she'd fallen into when she'd first met him. "Remember what I said. Don't wait. Live now."

I don't need you to tell me how or when to live. Hell, if it weren't for me, you wouldn't be alive at all.

There was no kiss, no embrace. He just stood and walked out the door. He stopped and studied Jay for a moment. "Take good care of her."

Jay squared his shoulders and stared back at Vince. His tone was matter-of-fact. "That's my job."

"Do it well."

"I always do."

Sarah paused to consider the step she had just taken. For the first time in her life she knew, without a doubt, she was complete unto herself and would be just fine without a man. After a moment, she took a deep breath and smiled.

Jay walked into the room and touched her arm. "Are you all right?"

She nodded. "I think so." She looked for the old feelings of rejection and inadequacy but couldn't find them. "I just lost a diamond."

Jay reached for her left hand and examined the spot where the ring used to be. His eyes opened wide and he pointed to Vince who was well out of earshot. "That guy?"

She smiled. "Yeah."

Jay looked in the direction of the door and then looked Sarah over with a grin. "If you ask me, he's a bloody wanker." He kissed her hand and flashed a smile. "Come on then. Let's go have a drink."

"Now that's the smartest thing I've heard all day."

She followed Jay downstairs and sat in one of the corner booths while he walked up to the bar and ordered. He came back and sat beside Sarah. A waitress followed shortly with three shots and a glass of water. The shots had to be tequila by the look of the salt shaker and the limes resting on the shot glass rims.

Sarah grinned at Jay. "That's great but what are you having?"

He picked up the glass of water and raised it in a toast. "Cheers."

Sarah took a lime off a shot glass, unceremoniously clinked the glass with his and tossed the tequila back like water on a hot day.

The amber liquid was smooth and warm. Definitely top shelf. Like liquid sunshine, it warmed her throat and then spread likes bright rays throughout her body from her empty stomach.

Jay smiled at her. "You took that like a professional."

"This isn't my first time."

"Breaking up or drinking tequila?"

Sarah took the lime off another shot and drank. "Both." She savored the warm feeling spreading throughout her body and smiled a Jay.

Yes, uncomplicated is better.

Jay rubbed his stubbled chin. "I find the first one hard to believe."

"Oh, believe it, Jay." Sarah relaxed as the tequila worked its warm magic. She lifted the last shot in a salute. It went down like lukewarm water.

How pathetic am I? I changed my body, my whole life, and I'll still end up alone. Oh, well. Fuck that self-pity crap. I'm gorgeous and rich.

Jay squinted at Sarah as though he were deep in thought. He leaned closer and whispered in her ear. "You aren't a drug dealer, are you?"

His breath on her cheek made her tingle. Sarah turned to face him. He was a good looking guy, even with the stubble. Good chin, nice lips that seemed inviting, strong jaw, mesmerizing eyes. His hairline was receding and the hair on his chin was no more than stubble. All together, it was an attractive combination.

He's here and he's a very attractive man. It would be so easy to move a couple inches and kiss him. I just want to kiss somebody and get rid of the taste of Vince.

Attraction aside, Sarah knew Jay could be trusted with the information and felt he deserved to know this was a C.I.A. operation. "Jay, I'm no more a drug dealer than you."

He stood and reached for Sarah's hand, smiling. "Okay, that's it. We're leaving now."

Oh, boy. This could be very good or very bad. I should have kissed him when I had the chance.

Sarah took his hand. It was warm and sure and in charge. She found comfort in that. As they walked past the bar toward the door, she pulled Jay to a stop and fished a hundred dollar bill from her purse. She dropped it on the bar and spoke in Russian as she pointed to the top shelf. "Give me that bottle of Patron."

The bartender snatched the tequila off the shelf and handed it to Sarah before grabbing the hundred. "Spaceba!"

Sarah grasped the bottle around the neck and smiled at the bartender. Maybe Jay assumed she didn't drink much tequila and she wasn't about to tell him three shots only made her warm in the tummy, but she'd just walked away from the man she had thought was the love of her life. What hurt was the fact that it didn't hurt.

Jay opened the club door, helped her across the icy sidewalk and held her elbow as she stepped into the car. He closed the door behind her.

They drove in silence to the hotel and walked without a word to their suite.

Jay was the perfect bodyguard, escort, and gentleman.

Inside the suite Sarah set the bottle of tequila on the bar, tossed her sable coat onto the sofa, kicked off her shoes and stretched.

Jay took off his wool coat and lay it carefully over the back of a chair. He took off his jacket and folded it over the coat. Then he loosened his tie and unbuttoned the top button of his fresh, white shirt. He wore the same tie that she had admired.

She opened the bottle. "Will you join me?"

"Yeah, you'd better pour me one." He dropped on one end of the sofa and leaned his elbows on his knees, watching Sarah closely.

Tiny tingles raced over her. It could have been the tequila but she suspected it was just the feel of his gaze on her. Sarah turned on some soft music before pulling two lowball glasses from the bar. "Do you want ice?"

"Thanks."

She dropped three ice cubes into one glass and then filled both glasses halfway with tequila.

She walked to the sofa and handed him his drink. She sat, curling her legs under her and leaned against the arm on the other side of the sofa. Her gaze locked with Jay's the whole time. She raised her glass. "To keeping secrets."

He raised his glass and drank with her. "All right then, what's the story?"

"I work for the American government."

"CIA?"

"I can neither confirm nor deny. There's a major drug ring in Afghanistan that we're trying to take down. My job is to go in undercover, a mole."

"Do the other guys who work for you know about this?"

"Yeah. We've been working as a team for a while now. We've done several missions together."

"So why bring me into this?"

She raised her open hand and shook her head. "Outsourcing. It's the American way."

Jay smiled at the joke. The edges of his eyes wrinkled and Sarah lost herself for a moment in his smile.

Why do I feel so comfortable with this man?

"My story is plausible, but I need a bodyguard and the boys' faces are getting a little too well known."

"And you don't have a problem with doing this line of work?"

She raised a brow at him. "Oh, I've got all kinds of problems. That's what makes this job such a good fit." She took another drink and then pulled out a cigarette. "Do you mind?"

"Of course not."

She lit the cigarette. "You can get out of this right now if you want to." She blew the smoke away from him. "I can get another bodyguard and you can go work for some Hollywood starlet with less risk. You didn't sign up for this sort of thing. I totally understand if you want out."

Jay leaned back against the arm of the sofa and fixed Sarah with a wide grin. "Not a chance, pet. This is just starting to get interesting."

It was probably the combination of tequila, ending things definitively with Vince, and the fact that Jay did such a good job pretending to be her lover, but the more she looked at him the better he looked. "Questions?"

"What else are you authorized to tell me?"

"Not a whole hell of a lot. I should tell you there's a Russian mobster with a bit of a grudge against me who may or may not be onto where I am."

"How much of a grudge?" He raised his brows and a smile curled his lips. "Did you dump him too?"

Sarah pointed at Jay's drink. "I'll let you finish that before I answer. Jay slugged down the tequila and set the glass on the coffee table then leaned forward, completely focused on Sarah.

Sarah took a drag from her cigarette, exhaled the smoke away from Jay and took another drink. "I earned a price on my head by killing his number one arms dealer and all his bodyguards and then reducing his very expensive home to rubble."

He lifted a brow. "You did all that by yourself?"

"Well, not all of it. I let the guys help."

Jay rubbed his chin. "Quite unreasonable of the man, not getting over that." The amused wrinkles at the edges of his eyes appeared again. This time his eyes sparkled.

"This is your last chance to get out. If you stay now, we need a commitment."

He nodded. "Oh, I'm committed."

Sarah shook her head. "Frigging amazing."

"What's that, pet?"

"Men can so easily commit to jobs like taking on the Red Mafia and international drug rings but when it comes to committing to a woman, forget about it." She scoffed at the irony.

Jay tilted his head slightly and looked deep into her eyes. "I didn't say it was the job I was committing to."

Ten

Moscow

Vince studied the condensation on his cocktail glass, ignoring the naked woman dancing on a platform nearby. "Sasha, I need to find someone."

Alexander didn't take his eyes off the dancer. Someone like her, or does this have to do with your personal business?

"Business, not pleasure."

Alexander tossed the girl a couple bills and waved her away before turning his attention to Vince. "Who is the person? Do you have a name or two? Maybe I know them." He lifted his glass to his lips.

"Nikolai Federov."

Alexander choked on his drink and gasped. "Federov?"

"Yeah. Is he a friend of yours?"

Vince knew the answer.

"No friend of mine! If this were friendly business you would have simply called him. Shall I assume this isn't friendly business?"

"Probably."

A tall, leggy blond stepped on the recently vacated stand.

Alexander turned to watch her and grinned. "Federov is a kingpin in the Ivanov Organization. There are plenty of the Mikhailovich crew who wouldn't mind seeing him drown in the Moscow."

"Can you tell me where he lives?"

"My friend, I must warn you, bringing harm to Federov is good," he shook his head, "but to his family would be very bad."

"On my life, I would never hurt a man's wife or children over a complaint I have with him."

"And what exactly is your complaint?"

"He put a price on my head."

Alexander's white teeth glowed in the club lighting. " Really? How much? Maybe I should turn you in for the money, kill him myself and be a hero?"

Vince glared at Sasha. "You want to try?"

Sasha slapped him on the shoulder. "Of course not. Now, that wasn't very friendly of him, was it?"

Vince raised his glass to his lips. " You can see why I'd want the information."

"Of course. Meet me here tomorrow. I'll have it for you."

~~~

After cutting her first multi-million dollar deal, Sarah celebrated with Jay and their Russian associates over a seven course meal at Moscow's most exclusive restaurant. Sarah sipped a strong espresso, occasionally participating in the conversation around the table and always making a point of laughing as authentically as possible at Anatole's tedious jokes.

The wait staff began clearing the table of empty plates.

Anatole set down his coffee cup and leaned back in his chair, giving his swollen belly a rub. "We should celebrate with drinks. I have a club nearby. Shall we?"

The other men all answered in the affirmative while Jay refrained.

Sarah set her cup down and smiled. "That sounds great, Anatole, but I'm afraid we can't stay any longer." She ran her hand along Jay's thigh. "We have other business that needs attending."

There were knowing smiles around the table as Sarah stood and Jay helped her with her coat. Once she'd slid the sable coat on, Jay's hands ever so softly pulled her hair from under the thick collar and lay it over her right shoulder.

His lips gently grazed the left side of her neck.

She gasped at the unexpected delight. The feel of his hands sliding down her shoulders and arms sent chills up her spine. His touch sparked every hot spot on her body into high alert. *Looks like another cold shower tonight. Damn.*

One of Anatole's bodyguards stood against the wall leering at Sarah and spoke in Russian under his breath as she walked by.

She whirled and slapped him hard across his cheek.

Jay had stopped immediately and turned to glare at the man. Sarah spoke loud enough for the whole party to hear. "I have entirely too much brain for someone like you to fuck it out." She sniffed the air to make her next point. "Besides, I prefer my lovers clean, wealthy and respectful in public. You are none of those and wouldn't stand a chance with my dog." She turned to walk away.

"You bitch!" He grabbed her arm.

She reached under her thick sable lapel with the other, and in one fluid movement swung back to him with a knife to his throat only a split second before Jay nailed him to the wall with a gun to his ribs.

Sarah pushed the blade close to the man's skin so his slightest movement against her would cut him. She glanced over her right shoulder at Anatole and then over her left at the others they'd had dinner with. No one spoke. She nodded to Jay, hoping he'd understand she had to be the hardass this time. "Thank you, Jay."

The big man's chest heaved and Sarah watched his pupils dilate. *Yes, be afraid. Be very afraid.*

Jay holstered his weapon under his arm, took a deep breath and one slow step back, eyeing the thug closely. Jay's contempt was apparent in his stance and focus.

Sarah pressed the knife-blade firmly against the guy's neck and pushed hard enough to cause him to lift his head. "Was there something else you wanted to say to me...*bitch*? Maybe you wanted to apologize for grabbing me? Maybe you thought you should apologize for disrespecting my escort, who I might add is more man than you'll ever be?" She pressed the blade against his jugular, a microgram of pressure away from breaking his skin.

"Excuse me. I'm sorry." He said through clenched teeth. "Please accept my apology."

Sarah paused to enjoy letting him sweat a few seconds longer and slid the knife back into its sheath under her sable collar. "Now that's better."

She forced herself to remain calm with a deep breath walked over to Anatole, speaking in a soft, low voice as she pulled her gloves on and briskly chopped the fingers of the opposite hand between each finger with a bit more gusto than most women might. "I'm sorry about that but if your dog so much as sniffs me again, all deals are off."

Anatole's mouth hung agape. Surely he wasn't used to people holding his bodyguards at knifepoint, especially women. "I'm very sorry. Nothing like this will ever happen again. Please accept my most sincere apologies."

Jay stepped up to the thug, who stood still against the wall. "She also likes her men to be tougher than she is, another reason you wouldn't make the cut, Comrade."

Sarah watched as the Russian, still breathing heavily, his face red, threw a punch at Jay who dodged the meaty arm and threw a punch straight to the big guy's face. The Russian dropped to the floor in a heap.

Jay stood over him as he slipped his hands into his driving gloves. "You touch her again and I'll kill you myself." He turned and reached his arm around Sarah's waist, leading her out of the restaurant.

Sarah chided herself for being thrilled at the macho display Jay had just put on, but it had been perfect for their reputation and would likely be good for business, not to mention making her hot as hell for Jay. She didn't say a word as he escorted her to the car.

Jay opened Sarah's door and waited for her to slide in.

She remained the picture of calm as she bounced up and down inside, ready to pop.

Jay climbed into the driver's seat and turned to her, beaming, as he closed and locked the door. "You were *absobloodylutely* amazing in there!"

"Me? Jay, you were incredible!"

He shrugged. "Just playing my part. I couldn't let you have all the fun. Bit emasculating having one's girlfriend be the tough one all the time."

Sarah touched his hand and leaned closer. "Was I too butch?"

He shook his head but kept his gaze on hers. "No, you were nothing but sexy."

"Sexy? I'll tell you what's sexy. You took that monster down with one punch." She was so pumped with adrenaline that her next thought flew right out of her mouth. "I think I had a little orgasm right then and there." Sarah stopped herself too late.

Whoops!

Jay didn't say a word, he just smiled.

The moment was perfect for a kiss. Blood rushed to Sarah's face. "We'd better get out of here."

Jay shook his head, breaking his stare and started the car. "Right."

~~~

Sarah counted all of ten customers and one bartender as she and Jay walked into Katarina's Bar. Most of the tables were empty. Two men sat at the long bar. It was a manageable crowd if something went sideways. She didn't like the idea of meeting an informant in public but this place seemed out of the way enough to not arouse any suspicion.

Jay chose a table near the wall with equal views of the front and back doors. "I still don't like this. We should have chosen the location. This place looks a little too cliché to me. It could be a set up by Nikolai."

Sarah sat in the chair Jay held out for her. "Giselle, our asset in Morocco, trusts this source and said this was a safe place to meet. I believe her. She hasn't led me wrong yet."

As soon as they were seated, Rig walked in and sat at the bar.

The hairs on the back of Sarah's neck stood up. Rig hadn't been part of the plan. This was supposed to be a simple meeting with an informant to get information on how solid Sarah's position was as Giselle's replacement with the Russians.

Jay looked at Sarah with a furrowed brow. "Which one is he?"

Sarah leaned in close to whisper in Jay's ear and his woodsy aftershave distracted her for a second as she breathed it in. "That's our guy, Rig. He swaggers. The boys must have found some intel. He's alone so he could only be here as bait. Something more than we'd planned is going down here. Be ready."

Sarah touched her ear to be sure she had the tiny earpiece in that she'd always used to contact Chris during their operations. It was still there. "Chris? What's going on?"

No response.

A young, slightly built blond man, perhaps only twenty or twenty-one, walked in and took a seat at Sarah and Jay's table. He smiled. "I'm Marton. Giselle told me to get in touch if I heard anything about you."

Sarah smiled at the pretty young man.

No doubt he's one of Giselle's many boy toys.

How did Giselle manage to keep so many men on a string? Hell, I can't even keep one.

"Thank you, Marton. I appreciate your help."

"Word of what you did at the restaurant last night has spread like fire through the streets of Moscow. Everyone in the Mikhailovich organization, except the brute of course, is very impressed with both of you. Anatole wants to marry you!"

Sarah nodded to Jay. "Well, that explains all the flowers and social invitations this morning."

"There's more. They found out someone in the Ivanov Organization, Nikolai Federov, has put a price on your head."

"And how much sway does the Ivanov organization have over the Mikhailovich right now? Are we in danger here?"

"None that I know of. Any enemy of the Ivanov is a friend of the Mikhailovich. The Mikhailovich heard about why there is a bounty on your head and they're ecstatic to be doing business with you. They call you the Black Widow."

"Really? Is that so?" Sarah pursed her lips, all the while smiling inside at what this would do for her credibility as a player. *If I'm going to do something, I might as well do it well.*

"Yes."

"Can you tell me why the two families don't get along?"

"A kingpin of the Ivanov had some of his new men rob a bank of the Mikhailovich some time ago. They've been enemies ever since."

"That's good then?"

"Yes, because it was the same man who wants you dead, Nikolai Federov. But you must understand, for as happy as the Michaelovich are to be doing business with you, the Ivanov are aware you're in Moscow. Your bounty is high. There will be assassins tracking you."

Sarah nodded. "I expected that would happen. Who owns this bar?" She could feel Jay watching her and saw him taking in all the information.

"Oh, this is a Mikhailovich neighborhood."

Jay's attention seemed to shift as two men in roomy black leather jackets walked in through the back door and looked around the bar menacingly. Jay nodded to Sarah.

Sarah noticed they made no secret of the forty-fives in shoulder holsters under their jackets.

Marton's face registered a moment of fright. "They're Ivanov men." Marton walked quickly out the front door along with about six other patrons.

Sarah leaned toward Jay so as not to be heard. "Chris, now would be a good time to tell me what the hell is going on here."

Jay watched her as though waiting to hear what Chris might say.

She shook her head. "Still no response."

The two thugs walked directly toward Rig and never gave Sarah a second glance. "You have some balls, Hennessee."

Rig appeared nonchalant as he glanced at his watch, then his crotch, and shrugged slightly. "Yeah, I do." Rig appeared the same prick he was when Sarah met him.

Was he that stupid or was it part of the plan to provoke these men?

Sarah checked her phone under the table for information from Chris.

"Don't make trouble, Hennessee. Come with us now. Nikolai has been looking for you."

"Sorry, I can't. I'm waiting for a friend. Have a drink. You can wait with me."

"You don't have any friends here." The flanked him at the bar.

"Oh, you'd be surprised at the places where I have friends."

The larger of the two men tried to grab Rig but the twin slipped free.

The smaller man threw a punch at Rig who dodged but didn't fight back.

"You gotta do better than that, Nancy."

The big man threw a punch that connected and they both tackled Rig.

The rest of the patrons stampeded out and the bartender hopped into a back room and closed the door.

Sarah thought she heard a lock on the door to the back room.

Chris finally texted. "Your earphone inop. Cavalry delayed. Please assist."

"Oh, shit!" Sarah shed her coat.

Rig was putting up a good fight but it appeared the men, who both outweighed him by at least fifty pounds, would finish him quickly.

Sarah put a hand on Jay's arm. "We have to help him."

"I'm paid to protect you not fight for some guy who's obviously made some tough enemies. He was looking for a fight."

"Fine, be useless." She jumped up. "My com is dead. Their plan hit the fan! Are you going to kick some ass or watch?"

Sarah shot into the melee and kidney kicked the man leaning over Rig. He grunted and crashed into a table on the other side of Rig.

"What the fuck? This ain't your fight, bitch."

Sarah punched the other man square in the nose. Blood flowed.

Rig tried to get up but three more guys ran into the bar.

One tackled Sarah from behind. "What do we have here? Two for one?"

As quickly as she felt his weight on her, she felt it lift and heard Jay's voice. "Can't let you do that, mate."

She turned just in time to see the man struggle and shout "Get off me!"

With a quick step, Jay bent the man's knee in a way no knee should bend. "Sorry about that. Nobody touches the lady but me."

She smiled at the comment just before dodging a punch from a wiry little man who was about six inches shorter than her. She smiled. "Well aren't you a cute little thing."

"Shut up, bitch."

There was a flash of flesh and sleeve from the little man's left and he tumbled to a small heap on the floor.

Jay had punched him in the temple. He gave Sarah an apologetic look and shook his head. "That's just no way for a wee man to talk to a lady."

Sarah caught the sight of two guys attempting to drag Rig out the back door. Panic shot another fix of adrenaline through her system. "You take the right, I'll take the left."

Jay sprung into action and the guy on Rig's right collapsed from a swift kick to his head while the guy on the left stopped as soon as he felt a warm stainless steel blade to his neck.

Sarah whispered into his ear. "Where's the car and how many guys are outside?"

"Sarah." Jay was standing beside her.

She tightened her grip. "I said how many are outside?"

"Nobody is outside."

Sarah pressed the knife to his neck. "Are you sure about that?"

"Yeah, we didn't expect anyone to help him." His voice went up an octave. "Oh, God, you're cutting me."

"Jay, would you bring the car around and help Rig in, please? I need to have a chat with this fellow."

"Don't be long, pet." He grabbed one of Rig's arms and pulled it over his shoulders while grasping the beaten and broken Rig around the ribs. Once Rig made it to his feet, they disappeared out the door.

"Don't take a deep breath. I'm a little on edge if you get my meaning."

A whimper escaped his lips. "You're c-c-cutting me."

"Now who's waiting out back?"

"Nobody. We left the car running."

"Let's be sure." Sarah walked him to the back door.

"Open it, but only a crack."

He did as he was instructed and there was an empty sedan, its motor running in the alley.

"Who sent you?"

"An important man who won't be pleased." He squirmed again and Sarah tightened her grip.

"A name!" Sarah let a few drops of warm blood trickle down his neck.

"Federov. Nikolai Federov."

"Okay, you get in that car and you go tell Nikolai that I'll be seeing him very soon."

"I don't even know who you are."

"The Black Widow." Sarah pushed the man out the back door then slammed and bolted it. She grabbed her coat on the way through the bar and dashed toward the front entrance.

Vince nearly bowled her over on his way in.

She didn't waste time on pleasantries. "You're late. Get out of here now and don't let anyone see you. We've got Rig." She gasped as she ran out into the icy cold night.

Jay pulled the Mercedes up and the passenger door swung open. She hopped in and then looked quickly to confirm Rig was in the back. He lay across the back seat looking worse for wear.

The car lunged forward.

Jay was all business as he shifted gears and watched the mirrors for anyone following them. "Where to?"

She considered her options quickly. If she left Moscow, she could lose face. If she stayed she could gain plenty of street cred but run the risk of getting killed in the process. "We aren't leaving town. Go back to the hotel."

~~~

Jay tossed the car keys to the valet and buddy carried Rig into the hotel the same way he'd pulled him out of the bar.

The front desk clerk gaped at the scene as they made their way to the elevator.

Sarah smiled and apologized. "Excuse us. My brother can't hold his liquor."

They rode the elevator in silence except for a few mumbles by Rig.

Sarah grabbed and filled a bucket with ice as they made their way quickly to their suite.

Jay unlocked the door and ushered Rig in.

Rig flopped into the first chair he stumbled to.

Jay pulled a bottle of cold water from the mini bar and opened it for Rig before handing it to him.

Rig cursed and took a sip.

Sarah dropped the ice bucket on the bar and retrieved a wet towel from the bathroom. She started washing Rig's bloodied face. "Did they break anything?"

"No. They just banged me up a little. I think my pride took the biggest hit. Not that I needed any help but where the hell was Vince? He was supposed to be there so we could take a prisoner." He winced at every touch of the wet cloth.

Sarah nearly snorted at his bravado. "Of course you didn't need help. Apparently Vince was detained. It happens more often than you might expect. Hell, on my first mission, he was about to get his head blown off when I found him." She dipped the bloody wash cloth into the icy water in the bucket.

Rig's turned his swollen face upward to look at her. "No shit? Vince?"

She nodded. "And no offense, Rig, but your pride needed a good hit. Just sayin'." Sarah dabbed gently at his left eye. "Now that eye is going to be pretty swollen." She filled a fresh hand towel with ice and handed it to him. "You'd better keep this on it for a while." She pointed to the door that connected her room to Jay's. "Go sleep it off in my room tonight."

Jay cut off what she was about to say next. "No need to put you out, he can bunk in here with me."

Sarah shook her head and smiled at Jay. "No, he'll be crying into his pillow about the fact a girl had to pull him out of a scrape. You need your sleep." She glanced back toward Rig and continued. "There's some aspirin in the medicine cabinet. Take a couple before you go to sleep. That'll help keep the swelling under control."

Rig stood on wobbly legs and looked at Sarah. Purple bruises were already forming on his face and around his left eye. "You do okay in a brawl, I mean, for a girl."

Sarah rolled her eyes. "Thanks. My trainer will be happy to hear it."

Rig gave her a hug with one arm. "You're all right, Sarah Stevens. I still think you're a bitch but I'm glad you're on my side."

Sarah smiled at him. "And I still think you're a horse's ass."

"Truce?"

Sara nodded. "Truce."

Rig gave a small groan and walked to Sarah's room. He stopped after a couple steps and looked at Jay. "Hey, thanks, man."

"Just doing my job."

"Make sure she gives you a good bonus." Rig walked into Sarah's room.

She heard him open the medicine cabinet and then turned her attention to Jay.

He had been watching her. A cut just over his eye was bleeding heavily. She tapped the seat Rig had been sitting in. "Sit down, Jay."

"Thanks very much." He opened another bottle of water and offered it to her before sitting.

She waved it off. "No thank you. You look like you could use a little though." She walked back to the bathroom for another clean, wet washcloth and returned, walking directly to Jay and leaning over him. She touched his head with her free hand.

He seemed surprised. "What are you doing?"

"You've got a cut over your eye."

He pushed her hand away. "Get that thing away from me, woman."

She stepped back, surprised. "Excuse me?"

"I'm the bodyguard, pet. I'm supposed to bleed. It's what men do." He grabbed the washcloth from her hand. "You, on the other hand are not meant to be banged up and bleeding. It means I've done a crap job."

Sarah paused, impressed with the pride he took in his work.

He stood, pushed her into the chair and bent over her to clean a cut on her cheek.

She took a deep breath. He smelled delicious.

"Did that hurt?"

"No. You smell awfully good for a guy who was just in a brawl."

"Thanks, the fragrance is a personal favorite. It's called adrenaline, sweat and blood." His eyes wrinkled at the edges and narrowed slightly as he smiled, continuing his cleanup. "You're not quite right in the head as women go, are you?"

She looked up at him and smiled back. "Nope. Not really. The scent works for you. You should wear it more often."

"I'll make a proper note of your preference for future reference." He chuckled. "You are definitely not like any other woman I've ever met." He examined the cut. "It's a superficial wound. Looks like a ring just missed the money. You'll be breaking hearts again faster than you can say Bob's your uncle."

"Great. I can't wait."

He looked into her eyes for a moment and quickly turned away. "I'm sure you can't."

Sarah opened her mouth to respond but he turned away quickly and peeled off his shirt as he strolled toward the bathroom. "You take the bed. I'll sleep in the chairs."

Sarah couldn't help but examine his back and arms as he walked away.

He's all muscle. Don't think about it, Sarah. It's just the adrenaline making you horny.

She tried to control the growing warmth between her thighs. "Don't be ridiculous. There's no need for that." She stood and grabbed the hotel phone on the desk.

Jay washed his face and then tossed the washcloth on the bathroom floor. He walked over to where Sarah stood.

He's a good looking guy even when he's sweaty and bleeding. He may even be better looking when he's sweaty and bleeding. Concentrate on the task at hand, Sarah. Jesus, look at those abs. I could scrub laundry on them.

He leaned against the wall and spoke in almost a whisper, a naughty grin overtaking his face. "Where do you propose I sleep then?"

Sarah dialed housekeeping, never taking her eyes off his naked chest. She raised a brow at him as the maid picked up the line.

"Housekeeping."

"Yes, would you send up a cot and some extra towels, please?" She hung up the phone and flashed Jay a satisfied smirk while attempting to pull her gaze away from his naked chest.

Jay was still beaming.

Does he ever not smile? Not that I'm complaining. Good God he's a charming son of a bitch.

"You did really well in there." He crossed his arms over his bare chest.

Sarah marveled at how muscular his arms were and yet he could wear a suit so well.

Oh. My. God.

"I have a question for you."

She nodded. "Okay, what is it?"

"Where exactly do you keep that knife hidden? And why do you need a bodyguard when you can so obviously handle any situation yourself."

Sarah kicked her leg up onto the desk and slowly lifted her already short skirt. "Tonight, I had my knife right here." She showed him the thigh sheath and no more.

He raised his brows and gaped, appearing duly impressed.

"I have a wide variety of sheaths and knives and always have at least one on me."

He shook his head. "Very sexy."

"I need a bodyguard because there's a Russian mobster who wants to kill me, and", Sarah pointed to her room where Rig slept, "Rig's twin."

"I see."

There was a gentle knock on the door and a soft woman's voice. "Housekeeping."

Jay grabbed a gun from the desk drawer and motioned for Sarah to stay clear of the door. He opened the door and a small woman in a hotel housekeeping uniform rolled a folded cot topped with two piles of fresh towels into the room.

Sarah tipped the maid while Jay casually glanced out into the hallway.

When the maid left with a smile and a nod, Jay locked the door behind her.

He took the extra towels off the folded cot and placed them on the dresser. He reached for the cot at the same time Sarah did, and when his hand touched hers, their eyes met.

She liked the feel of his hand on hers. She loved being constantly surrounded by strong, capable men, but she still longed for a soft human touch. She fought back the guilt of wanting to bed this man, knowing full well she was paying him to be here. He deserved a little more respect than that. She licked her lips.

I'll bet he's amazing in the sack.

"You did great in there, Sarah." His voice had softened.

"Thank you." She nodded. "You were pretty impressive yourself."

He shrugged. "Just doing my job."

Yeah, don't start thinking the people you pay to be around you are there because they want to be, Sarah.

It was time to stop fantasizing and get back to business. "Speaking of your job, after all this, do I need to look for another bodyguard?"

"No. This is a bit of fun. I'd like to stick around for a while and see what else happens." He stroked the back of her hand lightly with his thumb and she felt that gentle touch throughout her body.

Sarah remembered how she had become involved with Vince and it had served as a distraction during a couple of their missions. She knew she couldn't risk that again and slipped her hand from under Jay's.

"Okay, good. You can set up a cot, right? It shouldn't be too difficult. I'm just gonna go take a shower. I've got that early appointment with Anatole tomorrow and then we need to fly to Tangiers in the afternoon so it'll be a busy day." She quietly walked into her bathroom, careful not to wake Rig, and closed the door. She turned on the water and stepped into the shower before it warmed up. The cold water felt great on the bruises she'd acquired from the scuffle at the bar and it helped cool that longing she felt too.

I really need to stop being so attracted to the guys I work with.

Eleven

Moscow

The cool leather chairs on the private jet had never felt so good. Sarah collapsed into one and closed her eyes. She sighed at the abject luxury of it all. This was just one of the great perks of her job.

"Can I get you a drink?" Jay had removed his jacket and was pouring a glass of water at the bar.

"A glass of wine would be really nice."

Jay checked the bar. "Red or white?"

"Surprise me." She watched Jay as he chose a bottle of Shiraz from the cooler, opened it and poured a glass about half full.

"There you are, my pet."

He never breaks character.

Sarah played along. "Thank you, dear."

"Hmph."

"What is it?"

He sat in the chair across from her. "I rather liked that."

"You don't feel demeaned playing this role?"

"Not at all." He leaned forward in his seat and whispered so Rig wouldn't hear. "We could play a little harder if you like."

Her thighs warmed at the suggestion. "You always know just what to say to make me feel good." She raised her glass to her lips. "You may have missed your calling as an escort."

He winked. "There's still time, pet."

Sarah grinned and gazed out the window, enjoying her wine as they flew over Moscow.

The three hour flight to Tangier was quiet except for the occasional snore and snort by Rig. He slept the entire flight. Sarah suspected he'd had more of a beat-down than he'd let on last night and he had some recovering to do.

Sarah glanced across the table at Jay.

He reads the Russian paper every day. Intelligent, attractive, smart dresser...and a flirt too. I have to admit it. I really enjoy working with this guy.

Vince and I never really wanted the same things. The sex was good but there was hardly enough of it to warrant an actual relationship. Jason was right. I love the idea of being in love but I really love this job more.

She stroked her sable coat and admired her Rolex. She looked up to see Jay watching her.

"You enjoy this, don't you?"

"Private jets, sable coats, the best hotels, limousines, a gorgeous bodyguard and the opportunity to kick a little ass once in a while." She grinned. "What's not to enjoy?"

A smile crept across Jay's face and the corners of his eyes creased. His eyes sparkled. "So you think I'm gorgeous, eh?"

Sarah smiled, looking him over slowly and intentionally and then shrugged. "You aren't an eyesore."

He picked up his paper and opened it. "Nah, I'm bloody gorgeous."

Morocco

"Vince did what?" Will seemed furious as he pushed his plate aside on the table. Brian had grilled steaks for dinner on the deck of their yacht, anchored safely off the coast of Morocco.

"I don't understand what the big deal is here. A diamond ring is a contract to wed. We aren't getting married now or ever so I have no business keeping a platinum four-carat diamond solitaire."

"Nonsense." Jay eyed her from across the table. "You should be dripping with diamonds, engaged or not."

She smiled at him and chuckled. "Thanks."

Rig shook his head. "Stupid man."

Chris chimed in. "You got that right. If it had been my diamond, I'd have nailed it to your hand and made you marry me." He looked up in horror. "Did I say that out loud?"

Brian nodded. "Sarah, I just want you to know if you need a rebound guy, I'm your man."

Sarah chuckled. "Thanks, Brian. That's quite a sacrifice you're willing to make." She took a drag off her cigarette and admired the twinkling stars from her seat on the deck of their yacht. She loved the cool night air on the Mediterranean. "It's all right, really. I knew it wouldn't work."

Jason patted her on the back. "You know I'm always happy to take one for the team. Whatever you need and I mean *whatever*."

Chris sighed. "I think Jason speaks for all of us, Sarah. You're a hell of a woman."

Rig shook his head again. "Stupid, stupid man."

Sarah finally realized it was Rig saying it. "Rig, I'm flattered and a little surprised at you."

"What? I may be a horse's ass but I'm not stupid. I'd also be more than happy to be your consolation prize. You know, a great way to get back at a guy is doing his brother." He nodded like a bobble head.

"Thanks, but I'm a big girl and this isn't high school. I'm fine. I'm not hooked on the picket fence lifestyle anyway. I love the life I have."

Jay cleared his throat and stretched in his seat. "What's not to love? You've got private jets, sable coats, the best hotels, limousines, a gorgeous bodyguard and the opportunity to kick a little ass once in a while."

Sarah smiled across the table at him.

I love a man who pays attention.

"All right people, it is late and I'm tired." Will stood. "Good night."

"Yeah, I need to go contemplate the assholiness that is my twin."

Sarah chuckled. "Good night, guys."

Jason, Brian and Chris each said good night, leaving Sarah and Jay alone on the deck.

"They're right, you know." Jay stared off into the starry sky.

"Huh?"

"He's an idiot."

Sarah touched Jay's forearm. "Thank you, Jay, but it really is all right. When we left on this mission I knew it wasn't going to work."

"Really?"

"Yeah, that happily ever after stuff is a bunch of bullshit. It's better to just go for happily and be grateful for that."

"Not a bad idea, but I think there's a happily ever after for you out there." He put a hand over hers. "You've had quite a week. Would you like another drink?"

"No, you go ahead if you like. I'm going to get some sleep. Are you sure you want to sleep up here on deck? There's a sleeper sofa in my cabin." Her mind wandered to what it might be like to rip his clothes off and spend the night with him. She bit her bottom lip as a feeling of intense gratitude that he couldn't read her mind overwhelmed her.

He looked into Sarah's eyes. "No, this will be fine. It's been a while since I've slept under the stars. I rather miss it."

Such a professional. Never dip your pen in company ink, eh?

Sarah sighed, she knew she should learn her lesson about the company ink and stay out of it! "Okay, if you're sure."

Jay stood as she did. "Good night."

She wondered how his beard might feel against her cheek. "Thank you, Jay. Good night."

~~~

Sarah pulled her gaze away from the ceiling fan she'd been watching spin round and round as she lay in bed. She checked her phone for the time.

Two hours? What the hell?

She'd spent the past two hours tossing and turning.

I hate that he's doing the chivalrous thing and sleeping outside.

"This is ridiculous." She got out of bed and made her way up on deck.

~~~

Jay slept on the long vinyl sofa on the deck. His shirt hung open.

She leaned against the frame of the open glass door leading out to the deck and watched him for a moment, feeling a warmth inside she tried desperately to control before it became a fire.

His eyes opened and he smiled. "Am I dreaming?"

She shook her head. "No. Why don't you come with me?"

He sat up on the bench, abs rippling. "Huh?"

She smiled. "Come on." Sarah took his hand and led Jay down to her cabin. "You don't need to sleep on deck. I have a king sized bed, we can share. I trust you."

He stopped at the door of her cabin. "You shouldn't."

Sarah shook her head. "I'm sorry. What did you say?"

He spoke slowly and clearly. "I said, you shouldn't trust me."

A chill ran through her. She hated talking about trust while she was immersed in the word of espionage and double dealing. "What do you mean by that?"

"I mean you're a gorgeous woman and I'm not some *wanker* that throws away chances at gorgeous women. If you want to trust me, trust me on this, if I have the slightest opportunity I'll bed you and make you forget all about that other guy. I am not sleeping in that bed without having you. Now that you know where I stand, I suggest you let sleeping dogs lie up on deck." He turned to go but Sarah grabbed his arm.

"Jay."

He turned to face her and she stepped closer to him.

They wound their arms around each other and Sarah melted when she felt his lips on hers.

His shirt was already undone so she moved her hands to his shoulders and pulled it off, pinning his hands behind him for a moment as she did.

He ripped the shirt from his wrists and slipped the thin silk straps of her nightgown off her shoulders, pulling the gown down with a single, quick tug.

She stood naked in front of him, her heart racing.

He pushed her into the cabin and toward the bed without breaking the kiss that seemed almost magnetic.

The ache of desire shot through her. It didn't matter anymore that he'd been hired to protect her. It didn't matter that she might be on the rebound. None of it mattered because this gorgeous hunk of testosterone with the smiling eyes and rumble-strip abs wanted her now and she couldn't think of anyone better to make her forget about everything else and start living again.

Jay wasn't asking her to wait a few months, wait until the job was over or just stop doing the job she did. He was honest and forceful and demanding and she wanted all of him right now.

He grabbed her hips and threw her down on the bed. He dropped onto her, pinning her to the mattress. She could feel him, already hard, ready for her.

He stopped kissing her and propped himself up on his elbows.

She was all too aware of the hard length pressing against her, making her swell and ache for him, making her dizzy with need.

"I don't do this with clients and it's not on the bill. I want you. I've wanted you since I first saw your picture at Sentrion. Do you want me?"

All that flirting and joking around – he was serious!

She let her hands run down his muscular back to his hips, feeling every muscled inch of him along the way. Her hips arched upward as she answered. "Yes, Jay. I want this." She sighed. "I want you."

He bent to kiss her neck and her senses overloaded. The short, soft beard, the dark scent of him, the sound of his sighs, his hips slowly moving with hers was all too much. She reached down and fumbled with his belt.

"Oh for God's sake, take these pants off now!"

He looked up from the breast he had been licking, His gaze sleepy and satisfied, and smiled. "Oh, no. Not yet."

~~~

Sarah woke with a jolt. Her pillow was a fine, muscular, hairy chest.

Jay smiled at her and moved a lock of hair from her face. "You look delicious in the morning." He reached around her and pulled her close, kissing her softly and nuzzling her neck.

"Mmm…" She lost herself in the feeling for a moment. "Are you hungry?"

"Mm..." He kissed down her neck to her breasts.

Her stomach growled.

Jay gaped at the noise and laughed.

"Seriously. Let's go get some breakfast."

"Wait." He held her against his chest. "Do you regret last night?"

Sarah inhaled deeply and sighed. "No, Jay. I'd be a fool if I did. You were amazing."

He pulled her closer and kissed her again. "Good. So it isn't weird for you?"

She smiled. "Only if we don't do it again."

He rolled her over and pinned her with his lean, muscular body, already hard for her. "Let's take care of that right now. Breakfast can wait."

~~~

Brian looked up from his eggs and then checked his watch. "Where the hell have you two been?"

Sarah smiled at Jay.

Jay shrugged and pulled a chair out for Sarah. "Bonding?"

"Yeah, that sounds about right." Sarah slid into the chair and reached for the coffee pot in front of her, pouring a cup for Jay as he took a seat in the chair at the place setting next to her.

Brian stared at Sarah. "Sarah?"

She looked up. "What?"

He stared into her eyes for a moment. "Boo-yah!" He threw his arms up in the air. "Way to go, bodyguard!" He snapped his fingers. "Pay up, boys."

Groans were heard around the table as wallets were relieved of cash.

Jay shot a confused glance at Sarah. "What's this?"

Sarah sighed and rolled her eyes. The boys like to gamble and apparently I'm their favorite race horse. They took bets on my initiation test. And it hasn't stopped since. I'm sorry."

"No worries, pet. They're just jealous."

Jason handed Brian two hundred dollar bills. "You're a lucky man, Jay."

He laughed and winked at Sarah. "Don't I know it."

Sarah watched in amusement as hundred dollar bills and wads of twenties were passed to Brian. She'd come to expect this sort of behavior from her brothers-in-arms. She always seemed to be the subject of one bet or another amongst them. Oddly enough, Brian usually won them. She laughed as she remembered their very first bet on her. It had been during her final test to see if she had the mettle to be recruited onto the team. On her first day on the team, they told her about it and ever since then she'd demanded a healthy cut of any winnings based on her.

Brian smiled at Jay and handed him two hundreds and a fifty dollar bill. "Your cut. Sarah always demands twenty-five percent."

Jay sat back and waved it off with a big grin. "I already got my cut."

Sarah laughed.

He reached over and pulled a lock of hair away from Sarah's face.

Moscow

Vince sipped his hot coffee as he sat parked at the curb down the street from the address Sasha had given him, watching for someone to leave Nikolai Federov's house.

Federov was out of town, no doubt rebuilding the Arab compound that Vince's team had reduced to rubble while rescuing Vince from Federov's kidnapping attempt. Vince had taken some hard beatings on the orders of Federov, but the team arrived in time in a completely unsanctioned covert operation.

Vince didn't have to wait long before Nikolai's wife pulled out of the driveway in a gold SUV.

He started the Jeep Grand Cherokee he'd purchased just a few days earlier. He had to be careful what sort of car he drove into Nikolai's neighborhood and an upscale SUV seemed perfect. The last thing he wanted to do was stick out as a vagrant in a posh neighborhood in Moscow.

He followed her at a distance as she drove to a large fitness center.

Men and women walked in and out. Apparently it was coed. He followed her in and asked about memberships, listened to the sales pitch, and told the attendant he'd think about it. Then he went back outside to wait for Mrs. Federov's exit.

Within an hour she was back and on the road again.

She stopped at a flower shop so Vince followed her in.

He picked up a small bouquet and tried not to stand out.

When she had picked out her flowers, he stepped up to the cashier. "A woman should never have to buy her own flowers. Allow me."

"Thank you very much." She looked up at him.

She only stood about five foot six and had sandy blonde hair and brown eyes. She could be pretty with a little lipstick.

He smiled. "Haven't I seen you before? At the gym, maybe?"

"It is possible. I don't socialize much but I do exercise as much as I can."

Vince nodded. "It shows. Have a nice day and enjoy the flowers."

Before she could reply, he paid and left the shop. He hopped into his Jeep and drove back to his apartment with a smile.

Good work for one day. Tomorrow I go to the gym.

~~~

Vince stepped into the building, grateful for the warmth of the interior hallway, and stopped short at the delicious aromas wafting through Svetlana's open door. The last time he'd seen her, she'd been pretty beaten up by an ex boyfriend. The same guy Vince helped Sasha catch and kill. Vince peeked into the small apartment. "Svetlana?"

A pretty young woman emerged from the kitchen.

He hadn't expected her to be so pretty.

"Sveta, please. Hello." Her smile lit the room. "Come in. Come in."

Vince noticed just the least hint of the black eye she'd been given by the now dead man.

"Something smells delicious. Expecting company?" Vince couldn't help but feel protective of the girl. She seemed so sweet and yet she'd made such a poor choice in a man.

"Thank you. No, I'm not expecting anyone. I would invite you in for dinner but it looks like you already have plans." She motioned to the flowers in his hand.

"Oh, these? No, I don't have plans." He held the bouquet out for her. "They're for you. I wanted to see how you were doing and let you know that guy won't be coming around anymore."

She blushed. "For me? Nobody ever bought me flowers before."

"Then they are long overdue."

She took his hand and pulled him into the room. "You must come in and have dinner now."

~~~

Vince walked up the stairs to his small room, full from Sveta's amazing dinner.

He plugged in the electric pot and pulled the can of instant coffee from the cupboard. The water boiled in moments and he poured himself a cup. He collapsed, completely satisfied, in one of the chairs at the tiny bistro table in front of one of the two large windows in his room.

So that's what a normal evening looks like?

Vince was pleasantly surprised by Svetlana. She was a lovely dinner companion who didn't give a damn about world events. She was also an excellent cook.

Things with Sarah had been fantastic but never anywhere near normal. At least not the kind of normal he was looking for. From Las Vegas to yachts to mansions in Italy. It was all life over the top, and Sarah, she was a goddamned Wonder Woman, rolling with all of it. He'd only seen her break down once and who the hell wouldn't if they'd woken from a gunshot wound and found they'd won the lottery and become a millionaire while they'd been on the operating table?

Something in Vince had been screaming out for normal for so long. For one short moment he'd thought he could find it with Sarah, but that would never happen as long as they were both still involved in covert operations. He could see that Sarah had the makings of a great agent but that just wasn't the life he wanted. He wanted a home, a wife, kids running around the place, the whole domestic picture framed with a picket fence and a dog in the yard.

He was startled at the fact that he'd found the closest thing to normal he'd ever seen right here in Moscow.

He stared out the window at nothing in particular drinking his coffee. Snowflakes drifted downward and glistened in the weak streetlights.

I hope Sarah is getting along all right.

Twelve

Morocco

Sarah looked across the breakfast table at Jay. "How long have you been doing this?"

He set his coffee cup down. "What's that, pet? Having breakfast with a beautiful woman?" He checked his watch and smiled. "Eleven days, but I feel safe in saying I think I like it."

Sarah chuckled. "You're so charming. I meant bodyguard work."

"You're my second."

"How did you like the first?"

"He was old and fat and I didn't enjoy kissing his neck when I helped him on with his coat."

She laughed. "About that..."

"Too much?"

"No. It's nice." Her gaze lingered on him for a moment.

He picked up his coffee again. "Yes, it is."

Sarah's hot spots fired up again and she tried to breathe through it. "So, other than that, are the working conditions satisfactory?"

"First class accommodations, breakfast from room service every morning, a smart, sexy woman on my arm and the opportunity to knock out Russian blockheads in restaurants. What's not to love?"

"You didn't mention the pay. Should we be paying you more?"

"Don't you know?" He reached across the table for her hand and took it in his. "For you, my pet," he never took his eyes off hers as he leaned to kiss it, "I would do this for free."

Sarah gazed into his eyes and realized she didn't need this particular man in her life, but she definitely wanted him.

Moscow

"What a pleasant surprise." Vince threw a friendly smile at Nikolai's wife when he stepped onto the treadmill next to hers.

"Good morning. I never had the chance to thank you for the flowers."

He flashed a conspiratorial grin. "Shh. We don't want anyone thinking the wrong thing." He couldn't help but notice she seemed to jog a little faster and hold her shoulders a little further back.

I think she likes me.

"No thanks are necessary. I'm sorry. We haven't properly met. I'm Vincent. Friends call me Vika."

"My name is Natasha. Friends call me Tasha."

"May I call you Tasha then?"

Her cheeks went pink when she smiled. "That would be nice."

They both stepped off their treadmills a half hour later. "Tasha, would it be too forward of me to offer to buy you coffee sometime?"

"Thank you," she showed him her left hand, "but I am married."

All that money and the best his wife can sport is one lousy carat?

"Nice ring." Vince shrugged. "My mistake. I hope your husband knows how lucky he is."

Vince turned to go but he heard her whisper. "He doesn't."

Vince smiled and kept walking.

Got her on the hook.

"Wait!"

Vince turned with a grin.

"On second thought, Vika, I would love a cup of coffee. I know a nice shop just down the street."

"But your husband?"

"He is away on business. Besides one cup of coffee is nothing to be ashamed of."

Vince laughed. "It isn't like we're having an affair."

Tasha blushed again.

Yeah, she's ready for one though.

"I'll meet you outside?"

"I'll be waiting." Vince walked into the men's locker room, showered and changed. Tasha didn't leave him waiting long.

They walked to the coffee shop and Vince started asking probing questions disguised as small talk, all the while focusing his attention on Tasha and listening intently to everything she had to say.

She had three children by Nikolai. All away at the best boarding schools.

Her husband traveled often and cheated just as often. Vince managed to put that last part together pretty easily by the bitterness in her voice when she discussed his late night meetings and the fact that women called at the house all the time.

All clues led a man to believe she was getting pretty lonely by herself in that big mansion.

Ah, sweetheart, you are ripe for the picking. Don't worry, you'll be a wealthy widow soon.

Moscow

As much as Sarah loved a good meal, her Russian business associates really took the eating too far. Nearly every night this week, they'd been dining on rich foods that were adding too much of a burden to her already intense exercise regimen. If it hadn't been for great sex with Jay every night, she'd have porked out on all the extra calories. Sarah sipped espresso from the beautiful gold demitasse while discussing business with her Russian associates around the large dinner table in a private dining room in one of Moscow's finest restaurants. She heard the soft vibration of her phone and pulled it from her purse.

Jay set his drink down and watched her. "Important?"

She looked at the caller ID. "It's Marco."

Jay appeared concerned. "Not his schedule."

"I know." She flashed an apologetic grin at the table of Russians she and Jay were dining with. "I'm sorry. I have to take this."

Jay stood and helped her with her chair. "I'll come with you."

She shook her head. "I'm just going to step over to the alcove by the ladies room. I'll be back in a moment."

She answered the phone as she walked away from the table. "Yes, Marco?" Marco was the port manager that handled all of her shipping needs across the Mediterranean. He'd call her with regular updates every Friday on the week's shipping but today was Wednesday.

"There's been an accident."

"Explain."

"We lost a ship."

"What? In harbor or off the coast."

"About a mile off."

"Have the authorities been notified?"

"Not yet. I wanted to talk to you first."

"Good. My secretary, Chris, will call you with details shortly. Until then, no authorities."

"Of course, Scuro."

Sarah hung up on Marco and speed dialed Chris.

"I have a boat down. Can you call Marco for coordinates and get some divers in there before the product is damaged or discovered."

"Yeah, we can handle that, Sarah. Everything else okay?"

"Sure. I have a dinner I need to...argh!"

Someone grabbed her from behind. The phone slipped into her blouse as she struggled but she couldn't turn around. She pulled at the beefy arm around her neck as she was dragged through the kitchen. She gasped to speak, hoping Chris would hear her and track her with her phone's GPS but she could barely breathe.

Whoever it was, he dragged her outside and threw her unceremoniously into a car trunk, slamming it shut before she could see his face.

The car reeled out of the alley before she could find the interior trunk release.

What kind of idiot kidnapper leaves the trunk release engaged and my hands and feet untied?

She took a deep breath.

My phone!

She pulled the phone out of her blouse. "Chris, are you still there?"

"Jesus, Sarah. You scared the hell out of me. What's happening?"

"I've been kidnapped. I think Marco was in on it. I'm in the trunk of a car. I don't know how long I have before I'm delivered to Nikolai. Track the GPS on my phone and get Jay."

She hung up her phone to save the battery. As long as it was powered on Chris could track her GPS and give Jay the coordinates.

Now I just have to lie here in this trunk until something happens.

She took deep breaths to stay calm.

Jay will come. I can count on him. This will all be over in a few minutes.

Mere moments later she was thrown against the wall of the trunk as someone rear-ended the car. She smiled in the dark. "Jay!" She punched the trunk release and it popped open. She sat up and gasped when the cold night air hit her. Jay was motioning from the car behind her to stay down.

She lay on her stomach and braced for the crash that came about two seconds later.

The impact threw her into the corner of the trunk as Jay maneuvered his Mercedes to force the kidnapper's car in between two cars parked on the street.

Sarah had to blink a few times before she regained her bearings and tumbled out of the trunk. She stumbled to Jay's car and jumped in just as she heard two gun shots. She crouched down under the dash and looked up to see the driver's seat was empty. "Jay?"

He dived into the car and threw his gun on Sarah's seat. "Stay down."

She did as she was told and they sped off into the night.

Jay pulled his phone from his breast pocket and dialed a number. "I've got her." He hung up and slid the phone back in his pocket.

He looked down at her, still crouched under the dash. "Are you all right?"

She nodded. Suddenly she didn't feel so good. Her head throbbed.

"You're pale as a ghost, pet. Take deep breaths."

She gulped a lungful of air and wondered how she'd ever thank Jay for being so cool and fast, in this situation.

After a few minutes and several sharp turns, Jay stopped the car and reached for Sarah. "Come on up now, pet."

Her head throbbed."Owwww!"

Jay leaned over from the driver's seat and wrapped his arms around her, running his hand over her head. "No bleeding. There's a good bump. You could have a concussion." He looked into her eyes. "I'm sorry I knocked you about in there."

"It's okay." She breathed deeply.

"Are you all right? Do you know who I am?"

She reached out and touched the side of his face with her left hand.

"Yes, Jay. I'm okay. Thank you."

He pulled her close and kept his arms around her. "I'm sorry. You're safe now. I promise I will never let anything like that happen to you again. I'm so sorry, Sarah."

I believe you.

A flash of coherent thought ripped through the pain in her head. "Jay, you do know this wasn't your fault. They were tipped off."

He nodded. "I know."

"Do you know who it was?"

"Yeah. Remember that git I punched at the restaurant?"

"You think it was him?"

He put the car into gear and started driving. "I know it was."

"But how?"

"Because his brains are staining the passenger seat of that car whose boot you tumbled out of."

Sarah reached for the gun on the seat behind her.

"Don't touch it!"

"What?"

"Leave the gun there. I don't want your prints on it."

"The gunshots? You?"

He killed for me.

He glanced at her and looked back to the road. He spoke in a matter of fact tone. "I told him if he touched you again I'd kill him myself."

Wow.

She took a deep breath.

He didn't take his eyes off the road. "We have a problem, don't we?"

Sarah shook her head and took his free hand in both of hers. "You are the hottest man alive. How is it you don't spontaneously combust?"

"That's just the bump on your head talking." His eyes crinkled as he grinned. "Where to now? The airport?"

"The hotel."

Sarah pulled her phone from her bra and dialed Anatole.

"Da, Scuro! Where did you go? We've been waiting for you."

"Did you put him up to it?"

"What?" Anatole sounded indignant. "Who is this?"

"It's Scuro. Did you put your man up to kidnapping me tonight? If I find out you had anything to do with this, I'll let your opium rot in Asia before I ever let it move."

"What? That's ridiculous! Somebody tried to kidnap you?"

"Yes, your man from the restaurant. The one that grabbed my ass."

"I-I fired him that night. I heard he went to the Ivanov Organization." Anatole mumbled under his breath. "I'll kill him. I'll kill him now and have his head delivered to you by morning. I ordered no such thing."

"No need to concern yourself with that, Anatole. You'll find a car with two bodies, and an empty trunk at the intersection of Gosticknaya and Komdiva Orlova. I suggest you have someone clean it up with the police. And Anatole…"

"Yes?"

"I'll be at my hotel."

Sarah hung up, cleared her throat, and hit another speed dial number.

"It's me."

On the other end of the line Chris let out a low whistle. "Are you all right?"

"We're fine. Did you get all that?"

"Yeah, I got it all. Your boy Anatole is tearing up the night trying to find out if anyone else was in on this. He's clean. You should hear the chatter. He's shitting bricks. Most likely it was Nikolai's people. I've been tuned in to their frequencies all night and nobody has been on a phone that I can see. It's still silent."

"We know who it was. I'll email you from the hotel. Was Marco in on it?"

"No, I checked that angle with a local agent. That ship is down. Brian is on his way out there to supervise recovery operations right now."

"Okay, keep me posted."

"Will do. I'm glad we've got Jay there. He's quick on his feet."

Sarah looked over at Jay and smiled. Yes, he's very good."

~~~

Jay poured Sarah a glass of tequila as she collapsed onto the sofa in their suite at the Ritz-Carlton. The lights of St. Basil's Cathedral lit the night outside the floor to ceiling windows.

She watched as her fingers begin to shake uncontrollably.

Here it comes, the adrenaline crash.

Jay handed her the drink and she was horrified to hear ice tinkling in the glass like sleigh bells as she moved it to her lips.

Hold it together, you stupid wuss.

Jay stared at her, eyes wide with concern.

She flashed an embarrassed smile. "It's nothing. Just a reaction after the fact. It's a crazy coping mechanism. I'm fine."

Jay took the glass and placed it on the coffee table. He knelt in front of her and wrapped his arms around her. "You were amazing. To stay cool while calling Anatole and telling him off like that? I don't know any woman who could do that. That was the bollocks!"

Sarah hugged Jay close. The warmth and scent of his neck was too much for her to resist. She kissed him, letting her lips trail down below his collar.

He ran his hand up into her hair and gently pulled her head back just enough to kiss her fully on the lips.

It was slow and soft and Sarah melted against him. The familiar ache throbbed between her legs and she didn't want to deny it.

Jay moved his hands gently to her shoulders and pulled away from their embrace. "I'm sorry. That was taking advantage. In my defense you are rather irresistible. You just sit and I'll get our bags packed."

Okay, I'm embarrassed. Was that rejection or chivalry?

"No, Jay. We'll be safe here." She stood and picked up her glass, hands finally steady. "I'm just going to take this drink to my room and call it a night."

"Sarah?"

"Good night, Jay."

God help me, I would have had him right there if he hadn't stopped me.

Thirteen

Moscow

Vince balanced the two bags of groceries on one arm to knock on the door. "Sveta?"

Sveta greeted him with a smile. "What's all this?"

"You've been cooking for me for the past week. I thought the least I could do is cook for you."

"Vika! Haven't you heard? Men don't cook."

He set the bags on her kitchen counter and wrapped his arms around her. "You're in for a surprise then."

~~~

Vince sighed, satisfied with a good dinner and pleasant company. He sat on the couch in Sveta's apartment, belly full of good food, and Sveta snuggled against him as he watched the news.

"Vika?"

He looked down and kissed her on the forehead. "I thought you were asleep. What is it?"

"People need companionship."

Vince smiled. "Yeah."

"Do you still love her?"

"I'll always care about her but I don't think we knew enough about each other to truly love one another."

"Why did she leave you?"

"I told her to."

"Why?"

"Because I didn't want her to hang on to a dream that would never happen."

"And what about you? Are you still hanging on to a dream that will never happen?"

He wrapped his arms around Sveta. "With you, anything could happen. That's what I'm holding on to now."

"I don't need you to love me."

"What makes you say that? What are you talking about?"

"A woman needs protection, company and comfort. Love is overrated. Tell me you'll protect me, watch television with me and maybe warm my bed once in a while and I'll be content. I need no more than that."

Vince smiled. "I hope I can do better than that."

~~~

Vince and Sasha sat on one of the banquettes at Sasha's nightclub as Sasha explained his plan for a last minute vacation.

"Sasha, have you lost your mind?" Vince shook his head. "You're going to fly in crowded planes with uncomfortable seats for two days just to visit some shithole in the United States? Surely we have plenty of shitholes right here in Russia."

Sasha slapped Vince on the back, laughing. "This is not just any shithole, my friend. This is the mother of all shitholes. Las Vegas."

Vince's gut turned. Sasha saw casinos and strippers every day of the week. Why would he want to go to Las Vegas? "It makes no sense to me but I hope you guys have a good trip."

Sasha flashed a knowing grin, the same one that always hooked the ladies. "Not just us, Vika." He slapped Vince again. "You're coming too!"

"Oh, no." He held up his hands. "That's not a good idea."

"Why not?"

Because I'm a CIA agent. Because I'm supposed to be on assignment in Morocco. Because I need to find Nikolai Federov and kill him. Gee, I don't know!

"I don't have a passport."

"We'll get you one."

"The government won't issue me one."

"What government?" Sasha gave a dismissive wave of his hand. "I have a friend who issues passports to anyone. You take a picture, sign whatever name you like and pay the fee. You have a passport in less time than it takes you to eat a meal in the restaurant next door to his shop." Sasha stood. "Come. We'll go get some dinner and a passport. Tomorrow we leave for Las Vegas! Pavel is there. You'll like Pavel. He just opened a hotel. We'll be treated like kings."

Christ. This is going to be tricky. I need to call Will.

~~~

Vince had a bad feeling about this trip. He positioned himself in his seat, grateful to be in an exit row where he could stretch his legs, and buckled the seat belt around the ball of lead in his belly. He wished it was just from a bad meal but it was rock solid dread.

I'm known in Las Vegas and I'm supposed to be in Morocco. What if somebody I know sees me and talks to me? Where is a fricking drink cart when you need one?

He rubbed his forehead.

I'll just have to freefall off that bridge when I get to it.

Las Vegas

"Pavel!" Sasha seemed genuinely excited to see this guy.

Vince watched as a tall, grey-haired man turned around, wide eyed and smiling at Sasha. "Brother!"

They hugged, kissed each other's cheeks and hugged again.

Sasha kept his arm around Pavel's shoulders and directed him to Vince. "Pavel, allow me to introduce my friend Vika. He looked at Pavel and spoke a little less loudly. Vika is also a friend of Misha's and quite handy in a pinch."

Pavel looked confused. "Misha? Which Misha?"

"*The* Misha."

Pavel's eyes opened wide and he reached out to shake Vince's hand with both of his. "It is a pleasure to meet you."

"So you two are brothers?"

"We grew up in the same building. Our mothers were friends. Our fathers fought and died together." Sasha slapped Pavel on the chest and smiled wide. "Pavel taught me everything I needed to know about life, women and business, just like a brother would."

Pavel smiled. "I am so happy to see you here. Wait until you see the entertainment tonight." He waved at one of the desk clerks who practically jumped over the counter to get to him quickly enough.

"Yes, sir?"

"See that these men have our best suite. They are family and whatever they want, they get."

"Yes, sir." The young man snapped to and scrambled back behind the desk. He stuck a phone between his cheek and shoulder and spoke quietly but urgently as he typed into a computer. He returned in less than five minutes with room keys and a bell hop.

An employee standing by the front entrance waved at Pavel.

Pavel nodded "If you'll excuse me, I have a very important business meeting with someone who has just arrived. The bellhop will see you to your rooms. Rest after your trip. Order room service, whatever you like. When you are ready to go out tonight just ask anyone here where to find me. I'll show you the best time you've ever had." He slapped Sasha on the shoulder and smiled. "Good to see you, brother!"

Vince watched the scene between the two men. There was nothing less than admiration in Sasha's eyes. "Ah, that's Pavel, the big man." He glanced at the young man with the room keys.

"Gentlemen, if I may show you to your room?"

The bell hop loaded all their bags onto a cart and followed.

Vince watched Pavel as he walked quickly toward the front entrance. What Vince saw next stopped him dead in his tracks.

Sarah?

She looked amazing. She was dressed in her finest with legs up to there and shiny hair that seemed much longer than the last time he'd seen her. She was greeting Pavel. The bodyguard stood next to her, watching everyone.

Sasha saw her and as if it were automatic ripped off a wolf whistle.

Sarah glanced over at Sasha and nodded politely.

Vince caught her gaze through the crowd and nodded back.

Sarah ignored him and turned back to Pavel who led her to an office.

The bodyguard followed after giving Vince a hard stare.

Vince's hackles rose.

It didn't take long for you to move in on my woman, did it?

"Vika, come on!" Sasha's voice broke him from his thoughts of what used to be.

My God, she looks even better than she did just a month ago.

When they reached their suite the bellboy unloaded their bags and quickly disappeared after receiving a hefty tip from Sasha.

~~~

Vince set his knife and fork on the empty china plate and heaved a satisfied sigh as he picked up his wine glass in salute to Pavel. "That was the best steak I've ever had, Pavel." He looked out the huge windows they were seated near in the Carnevino dining room and admired the lights of familiar Las Vegas.

Pavel nodded, savoring another bite of the perfectly aged and seasoned beef left on his plate. "The best aged beef in the world, my friend."

Sasha elbowed Pavel. "Pavel, who was that beautiful woman you left us for this morning? Is she your mistress?"

Pavel rolled his eyes. "I couldn't afford her. Did you have to whistle like that?"

"Are you blind? Did you not see how beautiful that woman was? I'd have done more than whistle if I hadn't been so tired from the long flight."

"Sasha, have you heard of Scuro? Some people call her The Black Widow."

"Heard of her?" He nodded eagerly. "I tell myself bedtime stories about her every night before I go to sleep."

"Brother, that was her."

Shock registered on Sasha's face.

Vince watched with amusement as Sasha was struck with the reality that she was the woman whose stories he'd been telling over drinks. "No!"

Vince smiled. Sasha looked like a star struck groupie.

"Yes. That was her. If you see her again, show some respect." Her bodyguard has killed men for her.

"Yeah, right." Sasha was prepared to believe the legends about Scuro but a bodyguard never played a part in his fantasies.

"Do you remember Andrei?"

"Yes, Anatole's big guy." Sasha did a most muscular pose to emphasize how big Andrei was.

"Yeah, well they were all at dinner one night and Andrei did a stupid thing. He said something disrespectful to Scuro and she pulled a knife on him."

"She did? That's fantastic!" Sasha gushed.

Pavel nodded. "Then, not five minutes later, he threw a punch at the bodyguard and the bodyguard dropped him like a bag of potatoes."

Sasha looked incredulous. "But Andrei has at least six inches and sixty pounds on that guy she was with today."

"Had."

"What?"

"Andrei is dead."

"Mother of God! He killed him with one punch?"

"No. After the bodyguard punched him, he told Andrei he'd kill him if he ever touched her again."

"So what happened?"

Pavel pushed his empty plate toward the center of the table and nodded at the waitress who had been standing nearby. "He touched her again."

Sasha grinned from ear to ear and leaned in toward Pavel to hear the rest of the story.

"Anatole fired Andrei on the spot. Then Andrei and some idiot from the Ivanov hatched a plan to kidnap her and deliver her to Nikolai Federov. Federov has offered three hundred thousand American for her head. They threw her in the trunk of a car and were three blocks from Federov's offices when the bodyguard caught up to them, smashed their car off the road, and blew their heads off."

Sasha's chin dropped. "No."

Vince masked his shock at this story. Surely Will would have briefed him on this if it had actually happened.

Wouldn't he?

Pavel nodded. "It's true. There were no open caskets for their mothers."

"So how did anyone get the story?"

"She called Anatole right after it happened and told him." Pavel nodded for effect.

"So now she doesn't do business in Russia anymore?"

"Oh, but she does. She stayed in Moscow for three days afterwards and finished her business like nothing ever happened."

Sasha dropped his fork. He grinned as he slumped back in his chair. The look of admiration was unmistakable. "That woman has balls!" He cupped his hands in front of him to illustrate.

Vince laughed and nodded. He had to admit Sarah had the balls for the job she was doing. A woman like her would be wasted in suburbia.

Well played, Sarah.

Fourteen

Las Vegas

Vince rolled his eyes at the quick change in scenery. Not twelve hours ago, he was enjoying one of the best steak dinners of his life and drinking wine with Russians who loved talking about their businesses. When he got back to his hotel feeling no pain, there were two men in black waiting for him. He got the bum's rush into a black Town Car and was escorted to one of the office buildings in downtown Las Vegas where the CIA desk jockeys did all their pencil racing. He leaned back in the uncomfortable metal chair. The agent interrogating him was Steve Simpson, a total newbie. Vince remembered watching Steve's final test at the Camp. Steve had his ass handed to him which meant he'd never work in the field.

Agent Simpson rubbed his face and appeared a little more than frustrated with what he was getting from Vince. "Let me get this straight. You get yourself kidnapped by a Russian kingpin, break out - and I'm still not satisfied with your breakout story - then you get your twin brother to stand in for you during a top secret briefing and he goes on a mission for you while you go renegade in Moscow and infiltrate the biggest mafia brigade in the country. Have I got that right?"

Vince nodded. "Pretty much, Steve." He was in some of the deepest shit he'd ever been in but at least he had something of value to help buy himself out of the brig.

"Agent Simpson if you don't mind. So exactly how deep into the Mikhailovich organization have you managed to penetrate?"

"Why don't you be a good boy, go get me some coffee and then I'll tell you everything you want to know?" Vince smiled and nodded as if it might encourage Simpson to actually do it.

Simpson rubbed his neck. "We don't have any coffee."

"Seriously? You should do something about that. It would do wonders for morale. Our office has a Keurig." Vince made a clicking sound. "Very nice."

Simpson leaned back in his seat and pointed at the handheld recorder on the table. "Come on, Hennessee, we could have been done with this by now."

"All right, sport, but you know your interrogation technique is lacking, right?"

Simpson patted his own head like a monkey. "Aw, jeez! Just get on with it!"

Vince chuckled. He loved screwing with new agents whenever he had the chance. "I was brought in under the recommendation of the boss' father. One of the captains is a close personal friend of mine and he brought me to Las Vegas on a business trip to meet *his* close personal friend, Pavel Drugov."

Simpson's eyes opened wide. "The same Drugov who just opened the hotel and casino here on the strip?"

"Very good, Steve."

Simpson squinted, clearly annoyed. "Who set you up in Moscow?"

"A State Department connection."

"You have a name?"

"I do, but you don't need it."

"I disagree. I'm going to need all the names you've dealt with over the past month."

"Steve, why don't you look at what I'm bringing to this party before you start party crashing other people's careers."

Simpson laughed. "What have you got?"

Vince pulled his phone from his pocket and slid it across the metal table. "Recordings, photos and documents on Drugov's operation that are guaranteed to keep a crew of analysts busy for at least a week."

Simpson took the phone and walked to the door of the interrogation room, knocking twice when he got there.

The door opened from the outside and Simpson walked through, looking back for a moment with a sneer. "Make yourself comfortable. You'll be here a while."

Vince mumbled under his breath as the door closed and he lay down on the floor on his back for a little nap. "I don't think so, Steve."

~~~

"Mr. Hennessee, today is your lucky day."

Vince sat up from the spot on the floor where he'd been napping. "How's that?" Considering how refreshed he felt, he assumed it had been at least a couple hours since Steve had taken his phone and left him there.

Sasha will be wondering where I am.

Steve tossed his phone to him. "First of all, the agency is pretty excited about the information you collected. Nice work."

Vince looked at the display on the phone. Just a little past noon. He'd had worse mornings. "Thanks."

"Second, it seems you have friends in very high places. Do you know a Mark Davidson?"

Vince knit his brows and he squinted before nodding. "The name sounds vaguely familiar."

"Well, it seems he's your guardian angel. According to him you've been providing his operation with crucial information."

There was a knock on the door and a young analyst type, wearing the agency's black and white uniform stepped in. "Hennessee has a phone call."

Agent Simpson glared at the young man. "What?"

"Way above your pay grade, Steve. He's got to take it."

Vince stood and smiled his smarmiest smile. "You heard the man. Way above your pay grade, Steve."

The analyst type held the door open for Vince and pointed him to a desk.

Vince slid into the comfortable leather desk chair and sighed before picking up the phone. "Hennessee."

"Vince! How are they treating you over there?" Davidson's laughter was unmistakable.

"Aside from the interrogation room and no room service, just peachy."

"I've got a call in to the C.I.A. Director. They'll be letting you go in a little bit."

"Thanks, Mark."

"Any chance you'd take an assignment to Moscow? I could use more of what you've been getting about organized crime here."

Everything fell into place with that simple request. The only thing missing was an audible click. The life he wanted with someone like Sveta, the good he could do, it would all work together, finally. "When do I start?"

"Right away. As soon as they release you just go back to what you were doing. Tell them you got waylaid by some stripper. Oh…there's my other line. It's the Director. I'll see you when you get back to Moscow."

Vince hung up and scanned the room with a smile.

There it is. The break room.

He walked over to the break area, helped himself to a cup of coffee and flopped into a nearby chair.

Agent Simpson poked his head into the break area. "Mr. Hennessee, I'll need you to return to your cell."

"I don't think so, Steve."

Simpson opened his mouth to speak when someone shouted from across the office. "Hey, Steve, it's the Director's office."

Vince smiled into his coffee.

Nice job, Davidson.

Vince stood and watched Steve squirm while the Director of the Central Intelligence Agency spoke.

"Yes, sir."

"No questions, sir."

"Yes, sir."

When Steve hung up the phone he turned toward Vince. "I don't know how you pulled that rabbit out of your ass but you're released. Check in with Young and then report to Mark Davidson. You've been reassigned to a new handler."

~~~

Will hung up his phone and slid it across the dining table as Sarah and Jay walked into the company suite at Caesar's Palace.

Even though they all lived in Las Vegas, when they were undercover on the agency clock, they used this suite. Sarah's needing to meet with Pavel Drugov here in Las Vegas was an unexpected turn of events but not nearly as unexpected as seeing Vince in Las Vegas when he was supposed to be operating incognito in Moscow.

Will looked up at Sarah and loosened his tie. "The jig is up."

She shed her coat and draped it over one of the Chippendale chairs. "What jig? What are you talking about?"

Jason chain lit a cigarette as he paced the floor. "I knew that son of a bitch was gonna get made."

Brian sat at the other end of the dining table and rubbed his face with his hands. "What's the order, Will?"

"The order is we're all under investigation. Our current operation stops immediately. There's a car waiting downstairs to take us to the Camp and another to take Jay to the airport." He winced at Jay. "Sorry man."

Sarah's gut had a millstone in it. "After all the work we've done, intelligence we collected and the progress we've made on this case, now we have to go stand on the carpet in front of some desk jockey and get bitched out like a bunch of kids?"

"Pretty much." Will nodded.

"Bullshit!" Sarah grabbed a pack of cigarettes from her purse and rifled through it for her lighter. "Somebody give me a fucking light!"

Jason handed her his lit cigarette and she pressed it to the end of hers.

Jay looked around the room at each of them. "There must be something that can be done? Surely the government realizes you all work in the grey zone and rules are bent all the time?"

Will shook his head. "Yeah, they get that, but they frown on playing the twin swap game. We've got some answering to do for our actions and Rig needs to be debriefed."

"Well, what about me? I'm not C.I.A. Why do I get a plane ticket and Rig gets debriefed, which by the way" he glanced at Rig, "sounds very much like having ones trousers dropped and spanked violently."

"You were brought in with agency approval as a contractor on a need to know basis so we're all good where you're concerned. It's Rig that's the issue and yes, somebody's going to get their trousers dropped but it won't be Rig."

Rig stood from his seat on the couch and shook Jay's hand. "I just want you to know it's been a pleasure working with you, man. You saved my ass that night at Katarina's and I won't forget it. You ever need anything, you let me know."

Jay slapped Rig on the shoulder. "I'll keep that in mind, mate. Take good care."

Sarah took a hard drag on her cigarette. Anger seethed through her veins. "Fuck this. We all know this is bullshit. The Agency doesn't give a shit if we break the rules to get results for them, or cover their asses, but the minute we try to cover our own asses and protect ourselves from the dangers inflicted on us by our work they want to investigate us?"

Brian stood and grabbed his leather jacket off the back of the chair he'd been sitting on. "Yeah, it's bullshit all right." He walked over to Sarah and gave her a hug. "This isn't our first rodeo with investigations but you're about to get your cherry popped. We'll wait downstairs while you say your goodbyes." He shook Jay's hand. "Damn pleasure working with you, man."

"And you, Brian."

Will stood and shook Jay's hand. "You're a fine operator. I've enjoyed working with you."

"Likewise, Will."

Jason shook Jay's hand and gave him a one-armed hug. "Liked you from the moment I met you."

"Love at first sight, eh, mate?" Jay chuckled. "Take care, Jason."

Chris met Jay at the door. "You handled that kidnapping like a true professional." They shook hands. "It was a pleasure working with you."

Jay nodded and smiled. "You too, Chris."

Will, Jason, Chris, Rig and Brian left the suite and closed the door behind them. A porter waited outside for Jay's bags.

Sarah swallowed the ball of sadness in her throat.

I finally find a guy who's crazy about me and my life and I can't have him.

Jay wrapped his arms around her and smiled. "You'll be all right, pet."

Sarah sighed. "So this is it? Goodbye?"

He touched her forehead with his. "Is that what you want?"

Her voice was a hoarse whisper as she fought back the tears that wanted to come. "No."

"Good." He smiled. "We both travel a lot. We'll meet again." He touched her cheek with the back of his hand and looked into her eyes. "I'll see you soon." He ran his hand up the back of her neck and kissed her deeply, as though it may be their last. He pulled away after a long moment and gazed into her eyes. "We'll meet again."

She didn't move as he walked out the door without looking back. As the door closed, she choked on a tear. "I hope so."

~~~

Vince lit a cigarette as Colonel Young puffed on his cigar. In a world where smoking in offices was frowned upon, Young was old school. This desert training camp outside Las Vegas was his base and he ran it the way he wanted. His methods were unorthodox but they got results so the Agency never questioned what he did or how he did it. "Vince, I have seen you pull some stunts, but this one just beats the shit outa me. Are you aware that Will Adams brought your twin in as a decoy?"

Vince took a drag off his cigarette and picked up the glass of Scotch Young had placed on the desk for him.

Young ran a hell of an operation but his debriefs were never conducted the way the suits downtown did things.

"Yes. It was my idea and all my doing."

"You realize you could be in some heavy shit for freely admitting that?"

Vince nodded. "Yes."

Young glanced at his computer screen. "Looks like you brought in some great intelligence. What do you think you're going to get from the agency on this?"

Vince eyed the man who had left him out to hang when Nikolai Federov kidnapped him and took him to a compound in Saudi Arabia. A compound he never would have escaped from if his team hadn't gone off the reservation and mounted an unauthorized armed assault on the place. "I know better than to expect an apology, but a full pardon for my trouble and permanent reassignment to a new handler are reasonable requests, don't you think?"

"We could do the pardon, but I don't know about another assignment."

"I've already accepted one for a non-official cover in Russia." He drained the glass of Scotch and set the crystal glass on the desk. "You aren't my handler anymore."

Young glared at him. "As always you've got it all sewn up. Is that all?"

"I want my brother and my former teammates cleared of any suspicion of possible wrong doing."

Young leaned back, spreading his massive shoulders the width of the huge leather chair he occupied. "Considering the trauma you've been through and the intelligence you've been able to gather¼" He nodded, "I think we can do that."

Vince stood and extended his hand. "Thanks, Colonel." He had all the aces in this negotiation, but he could be a good sport about it. After all, Young had people to report to as well.

Young smiled and shook his hand. "It's been good working with you. Watch your ass out there."

~~~

Sarah pulled up her usual seat at the briefing table. After making the team stand by in a bunkhouse at the Camp overnight, Young finally called them in to the conference room. He took a seat at the head of the conference table and slammed his coffee cup down. It must have been empty because nothing splashed. "You people had the balls to try to put one over on the C.I.A.? I can't decide if you're all stupid, cocky, or just plain brilliant."

Jason snickered.

Young pointed to Jason and glared around the table at Will, Chris, Brian and Sarah. "This is totally off the record and needs to go to your graves with you. I'm impressed with your creativity and initiative but officially I have to reprimand you. The second Mr. Hennessee has been debriefed, compensated and written off as an asset but don't you ever try to pull something like this again or I'll kill you all myself."

There was a collective enthusiastic answer, military style. "Yes, sir."

"The first Mr. Hennessee has been permanently reassigned. Your next assignment will not include either of the Hennessees. Are we clear?"

Again, the collective response. "Yes, sir."

"All right, you girls stand by here while I speak to Stevens in my office. Smoke 'em if you got 'em." Young stood and pointed Sarah to the door to his office. "Stevens?" He followed her in and closed the door. "Have a seat."

Sarah sat in one of the large leather wingback chairs positioned in front of his desk.

How many hundreds of things could this be about?

Young sat on the corner of his desk facing her. "There have been some developments since I spoke to Will this morning and called you all in. We want you to continue the operation, to go back in and take over for Giselle."

Sarah shook her head in an attempt to shake the confusion. "I'm sorry. You want me to what?"

"We want you to take this assignment long term. You've been very successful in the short amount of time you've been in that operation and we'd like to take advantage of your momentum and post you in Tangiers indefinitely."

Holy shit! That's awesome. Okay, stay cool.

"Why?"

"Because we're very close to closing down the whole operation from Afghani poppy fields to Russian mafia. From Hassan to Victor and now to these Russians, we've worked it back to the source of Al Qaeda's funding. With you on the inside we can get everybody. We can round them all up. It's just a matter of keeping you in there."

So you need me now? Work for it.

"Why me? Why not keep Giselle?"

"Giselle is getting older and wants to retire. She's informed us that you've won over her associates and they'd be amenable to continuing business with you."

The agency needs me. This is the big score and they need me to pull the trigger. I see a bargaining chip or two here.

"Let me make sure I'm clear here." She leaned back on one elbow and fixed Young with a stare. "Giselle is bailing and you can't hold her.

You're about to lose the whole can of worms, not to mention a significant Black Ops funding source if I don't take this assignment. Is that about right?"

Young sighed. "I've always appreciated your ability to cut through the bullshit. We need you to do this but we need you to volunteer."

"Okay, I'll do it but if you want me to volunteer, but I have some conditions that could be deal breakers."

Young shook his head and bent forward, leaning on one knee. "Maybe we taught you too well." He grinned. "Okay, shoot. What are your terms?"

"First, I want my team with me."

Young shook his head. "That's impossible. Hennessee has already taken an assignment in Russia."

Sarah dismissed that problem with a wave of her hand. "That's fine but I want the rest of the team and I want my bodyguard back."

He nodded. "Absolutely, we'll assign a new member unknown in that area to act as your bodyguard."

"No." Sarah pursed her lips and shook her head slowly. "You don't understand. I want the bodyguard I had with me in Tangiers."

"The British freelancer from Sentrion?"

"Yes."

"We can't do that, Sarah. You could be in there for a while and he'll be privy to some sensitive information."

"So we bring him on as an asset. We'll brief, debrief, the whole nine yards. He's former S.A.S. He's been vetted. He's got the clearance."

"Okay, I'll tell you what. If you can find him and he's up for it, we can put him on the payroll and make it work."

Sarah smiled, excitement shot through her with every heartbeat.
Yes!

Young scratched his head. "Any other mountains you want moved or can we get this show on the road?"

Sarah sighed. "No, I can't think of anything else."

"All right then." Young stood. "You drive a hard bargain. Let's go talk to the boys."

Sarah walked into the conference room first, cocky as you please wearing a wide grin, and situated herself in her usual chair at the conference table.

Young started speaking before he crossed the threshold from his office. "Here's the assignment. This one is long term. With Sarah taking over for Giselle, we're poised to take down the major money source for insurgent actions in the Middle East. Sarah has agreed to the assignment with a couple of conditions, one being that you bums go with her. We need to know now if you're up for it."

Will spoke first. "Are we going to live on the boat or will we get a house?"

"Goddamnit! What is with the negotiators today? You agents are killing me!"

Will remained calm after Young's outburst. "I've got nothing against boats but they can get pretty cramped long term."

"All right, a house would be better for the security aspect. You'll keep the boat for transportation and logistics."

"Do we get to pick the house?"

"Yes, Chris."

"And cars?"

"Yes, Jason."

"How exactly are the rest of us going to fit into this operation if it goes long term?"

"The same way you have been, Will. Chris and Sarah will continue to gather raw data. You'll continue with analysis and Jason and Brian will focus on team security."

Brian cocked his head to the side. "What about Sarah's security? She's already been kidnapped once and there's still a price on her head."

"Sarah's other request was to have her previous bodyguard assigned to the operation as an asset. I don't have a problem with that if you don't."

Brian's mouth opened wide. He stared at Sarah but no words came out.

That's right baby, mama calls the shots now.

Sarah raised a brow. "Is there something you want to say, Brian?"

Brian caught his breath. "You da man!"

"Thank you. So are you guys in?"

Jason smiled. "A mansion in Morocco and personal security duty? Oh, hell yes."

There were nods around the table.

"We'd like you all in place in one week. Do you think you can wrap up your affairs and work within that timeline?"

Again there were nods around the table.

"Dismissed."

They had no sooner walked out of the building than Brian slapped Sarah on the shoulder. "You're the fucking man, Stevens! You made them give you your conditions on an assignment. Who the fuck does that?"

Jason put his arm over Sarah's shoulder and grinned his evil grin. "The Black Widow, apparently. You think you can get me a sports car?"

Sarah chuckled. "I'll see what I can do. Barbeque at Brian's and shop talk over steaks tonight?"

"Are you kidding? We've got travel plans to make, real estate to check out and Jay to track down. Good call on getting him on the case, Sarah. Very impressive." Will smiled. "It's exactly what I would have done in your shoes."

Pride bubbled inside her. "Thank you. I'll see you guys at eight. The steaks are on me."

~~~

Sarah walked into Brian's house with a bag of steaks in one hand and a bottle of Anejo in the other. "Honey, I'm home!"

Will looked up from the kitchen table as he set down his phone. "Sarah, I just spoke to Brock. We can't get Jay. He's already taken another assignment. I told Brock to send us another guy."

Sarah placed the bags on the kitchen bar, sat at the table and lit a cigarette. She paused for a few minutes, smoking her cigarette, while she considered what Will had said.

I'm not some dumb grunt. I've taken hits for this team and I've learned how things work. I'm tired of compromise and sacrifice. If I have to do this job I want Jay.

She took one last long drag and stubbed out her cigarette. "There's no such thing as *can't* Will."

"Sarah, he's in the middle of an armed conflict in the mountains of Afghanistan."

"Well then it's a good thing I have some connections there." Sarah pulled her phone out of her pocket.

"Sarah, I wouldn't advise this. You clearly have feelings for the guy."

She glared at Will. "Then I guess it's a good thing I didn't ask for your advice. Hm?" Sarah flipped open her phone and hit the speed dial for Brock.

"Brock Benjamin."

"Sarah Stevens here."

"Hey, Sarah. Will says you need a new bodyguard. Same specs as before?"

"No. Belay that order. I need Jay Stanstead."

"Jay's doing some contract work in Kunduz. He's in Afghanistan."

"I know where Kunduz is, Brock. I need you to transfer him back to me as a bodyguard."

"I can't do that, Sarah."

"Why not?"

"Once he's taken a job I can't pull him off it. He needs to initiate the request."

"I see. Get the paperwork ready. You'll be hearing from him soon." Sarah hung up and pulled up a map on her phone.

Chris looked over her shoulder. "Girl, what are you doing?"

"Chris, I'm not a pawn anymore. I'm a player with muscle and it is time for me to flex."

Brian sat at the table beside her and took a conspiratorial tone. "And so the student becomes the master."

Sarah dialed Anatole in Russia. She knew he dabbled in arms deals as a side hustle to his drug business. He picked up the phone and she switched from English to Russian like a native.

"Anatole, good evening. This is Scuro."

"How are you, Scuro?"

"I'm well but I could be better. What have you got near Kunduz?"

"I own Kunduz."

"Excellent. I'm in Las Vegas. I'll be flying out from the United States tonight. I'll be in Moscow in a couple days. I want a flight to Kunduz from there." Sarah pointed to Jason and Brian. "I'll have two security personnel with me. Can you make it happen?"

"That depends, will you give me a break on my next shipment?"

"We can discuss it, my friend."

"That's good enough. I'll have a plane waiting in Moscow that will take you to a helicopter with one of my pilots in Afghanistan. Call me when you're an hour from landing."

"Thank you." Sarah hung up the phone.

Jason grimaced at Sarah. "Two bodyguards?"

"I'm a female flying into a hot spot in Afghanistan. Anything less would be considered underdressed."

Jason shrugged. "True dat."

"Will, would you get us a charter to Moscow as soon as possible? You and Chris get to Tangiers when you can. We'll meet you there. I don't have any apologies for you, Will. I'm not doing this any other way."

Will smiled, stood and clasped her shoulders. "You really were paying attention. You've learned well. I'm so impressed with you right now I could just burst. No apologies required. You're acting like a real kingpin now and that's what we wanted all along."

"Jason, Brian, pack your tough guy togs. Will, can you have a car pick us all up for the flight tonight? I'm going back to the MGM to pack."

"You got it, Sarah."

"Hey, what about the steaks?" Jason looked sad.

"When we get to Tangiers, I'll buy you an Aston Martin to make up for it."

Jason perked up like a happy puppy. "Okay!"

Fifteen

Moscow

Vince settled into the back seat of the limo and stretched his legs. Sasha had ordered a limo for them at the airport after their long series of flights from Las Vegas to Moscow.

Sasha had never batted an eye when Vince told him his disappearance was due to a beautiful woman distracting him for a few hours. Sasha had been too busy living it up in Sin City to notice anyway.

When the car pulled up to Vince's building, Sasha smacked him on the shoulder. "Time to service your woman. She's probably waiting for you with legs wide open!"

Vince shook his head. "You can be a real pig sometimes, Sasha."

Sasha laughed. "That's why the women squeal for me!"

Vince grabbed his bag and stepped out of the limo, excited about what his staying in Moscow might mean for him and Sveta. He used his key and walked into Sveta's apartment. "Sveta? I have good news."

She didn't answer.

A retching sound came from the bathroom.

"Sveta?" He walked to the bathroom and cracked the door open. She slammed it quickly before retching again. "Are you still sick? I've been gone for a week now. We need to take you to a doctor right now."

"I've been to a doctor. I'm fine."

"No you aren't. You've been throwing up. That is not fine."

He heard her brushing her teeth so he grabbed his bags and put them in the bedroom.

She emerged from the bathroom wiping her face with a wet towel. "Vika, sit down."

This must be serious.

"Whatever it is, we'll get through it together, Sveta."

"A baby isn't really something you get through, Vika."

He nearly stumbled onto the couch. "A baby?"

She nodded as she sat and took his hands in hers. "Please don't be angry."

The blood rushed from Vince's head and dreams of a family rushed in.

A baby. I'm going to be a father.

"Sveta, angry? I'm so happy I can't breathe." He put his hand on his chest. "Do you have any idea how thrilled I am?" He wrapped his arms around her in a big hug and kissed the top of her head. "You have made me happier than any woman ever has."

He reached into his pocket for the ring he'd been too unsure to present until now. He knelt before her and held out the four-carat diamond solitaire. "Marry me."

Sveta gasped at the sight of the ring. "Really?"

He nodded and slipped the ring on her shaking finger.

"Yes."

A family. Finally. Who knew I'd find normal so far from home.

~~~

Vince shared the good news with Sasha at his club that night. Sasha conducted all of his business at Rasputin now and had started having Vince attend his meetings. It was clear Vince was under Sasha's wing now.

Sasha toasted Vince's good fortune and smiled the way he always did before launching into one of his tall tales.

Vince chuckled knowingly. "What's it going to be this time?"

Sasha glowed. "So my friend who usually flies arms and ammunition picks up three passengers at an old air base outside Moscow. They pull up in an armored Mercedes and out come two big American brutes and this knockout brunette with green eyes. They have no luggage but they're all packing under their jackets. You know?"

Vince took a sip of his drink. "It turns out she's going to Afghanistan and these brutes are her bodyguards. She's some hotshot who's connected with my friend's boss through her business."

"What's she do?"

"She's the biggest opium transporter in the world."

"What's her name?"

Sasha stretched his arms wide. "Scuro, of course! So they land the plane in Afghanistan and swap it for a Sikorsky and fly toward Kunduz when my friend sees a skirmish in the valley below. He moves to avoid it and that's when things get really weird."

Afghanistan

Sarah had a bad feeling about what she saw going on below. Guys from three beat-up trucks appeared to be moving in and firing at people in a single, newer model truck. This was no carjacking. She pulled out the binoculars from a pocket beside the seat and peered at the newer truck while the pilot changed the Blackhawk's course away from the action. A chill ripped up her spine.

Jesus! It's Jay!

"Go back! Pilot, go back!"

The pilot shook his head. "No way! They might have rockets."

Sarah pulled the sidearm from her thigh holster, locked a round into the barrel of her .45 and tapped the pilot's helmet with it. "I'd be more concerned about what the crazy bitch in this helicopter has if I were you. I said go back." She tapped his helmet one more time for emphasis. "Now do it. You've got plenty of firepower. Engage and destroy those trucks."

"Uh, Sarah…are you sure you want to do that?" Brian whispered.

Sarah glared back at Brian. "We're going back there now. I don't care if he flies this rig or one of you do. I'd do no less for any of you. That man down there saved my life. Now we can return the favor."

Jason smiled wide as he scrambled into one of the gunner seats. "I'd give my left nut to have a woman like you."

Sarah didn't flinch. "A woman like me would cost you both of them."

Brian nodded at Jason and slid into the other gunner position to check his weapon.

Sarah nodded to the pilot. "Now let's see what you've got."

The pilot made a wide turn and flew low and fast back toward the fray below.

Jason and Brian opened fire with the mini-guns and reduced the beat up trucks to charred heaps within seconds.

Sarah watched Jay and his partner use the distraction to their advantage. They scrambled back into their truck and hauled ass out of there.

Sarah holstered her handgun and leaned back in her seat. "Follow that truck. That's where we're going."

Moscow

Sasha took another sip of his drink while Vince waited for more of the story. "So my friend follows the truck and lands in this mercenary camp. Scuro apologizes for hijacking him and gives him one thousand American dollars for his trouble. By now, my friend is so hard for this bitch he can't even think straight so he takes the money and waits with her bodyguards in the chopper while she struts into that camp, bold as brass. How crazy is that?"

Vince suspected Sasha would fall into a dead faint if he ever met Sarah in person and wondered if he should arrange it just for kicks.

Sasha's eyes gleamed as he continued his story.

Afghanistan

Sarah stepped out of the chopper as Jay and his partner were walking toward it.

He looked rough. The beard was longer, his face looked haggard, and his clothes were dirty. None of it mattered.

She caught her breath and smiled.

Jay's face lit with a broad smile and he walked a little faster toward her.

Relief washed over Sarah. She'd found him again. This time she wouldn't let him go.

He grabbed her around the waist. "Guns blazing and looking like a million bucks. Woman, you have got style. What the bloody hell are you doing here?"

"They want me to stay on the case. I need a good bodyguard and this shithole doesn't suit you."

"Well, you were moments away from being out of a bodyguard as we were nearly out of ammo. You saved my fucking ass!" Jay picked her up in a bear hug and kissed her hard. He pulled away and looked her in the eyes. "Is there anything you *can't* do?"

"I can't make you come with me."

"And leave all this?" He laughed. "You flew to the bloody end of the earth for me and saved my ass with your perfect timing. You'd have to shoot me now to stop me from following you!"

Sarah wrapped her arms around him and hugged him close. "Not a chance."

He pulled away slightly. "Is this purely business?" He grinned. "I'll expect my previous benefits package." He pulled her close and nuzzled her neck.

"I want it all. The job, the lifestyle and you."

"That sounds like a winning combination to me, pet, but I can't just bail. I have to stay until a transfer can go through."

Sarah pulled out her phone and hit the speed dial for Brock. "I don't think that will be an issue." She put the phone to her ear. "Brock! Good morning."

"It's the middle of the night here, Sarah."

"It's morning in Kunduz. You got that paperwork ready?"

Brock's voice cracked slightly. "Are you serious?"

Sarah handed the phone to Jay. "You want the transfer?"

Jay took the phone. "Brock, its Jay. You'll never believe what just happened here. I'm picking up that bodyguard gig again."

Jay nodded as he listened. "Yeah, I know. But the working conditions are brilliant." He laughed. "Right. Thanks, mate." Jay hung up the phone. "Let me get my gear and we'll get out of here."

Moscow

Sasha took one final gulp of his drink and set the glass on the table.

One of the waitresses was there to pick it up immediately.

"Another?"

"Not now." He waved her away. "So Scuro picks up this guy and they all fly back to the airfield and then hop a private jet back to Moscow the same day. My friend said he made an extra five thousand that day. I think he would have done it free for a night with Scuro."

151

"She must be one hell of a woman."

"Are you kidding? You saw her! She's gorgeous and has bigger balls than most men. I'd leave my wife and my fortune for a woman like that."

I'm sure you would.

"I had a woman like that once."

In fact, I had that woman and, yeah, she'd have been worth a free flight through a hot zone.

"What did you do to make her leave you?"

Vince considered. "We wanted different things. Her career was very important to her and I couldn't ask her to leave it."

Sasha smacked Vince on the back of the head. "What? A woman like Scuro, with a career too? You never leave a woman like that. That's the Holy Grail, you fool."

"Don't I know it." Vince considered Sasha's words. He knew Sasha would love everything about being involved with a woman like Sarah, but Vince had a different life in mind for himself.

~~~

Vince made his way home after a long night spent toasting his good fortune and his fiancé. He'd just knocked on Sveta's door when he heard a noise upstairs like a door swinging open and bouncing off the wall.

A woman's voice screamed "Vika!" and was quickly muffled.

"Linka?"

Sveta appeared at the door. "Vika, what's wrong?"

Vince pulled the gun from his belt and charged a round before taking the stairs two at a time. He shouted over his shoulder. "Lock your door, go to the bedroom and call Sasha!" When he came to the last flight of stairs, he peeked at Linka's door through the rails and saw Nikolai holding Linka by the neck from behind.

She seemed almost apologetic. "Vika, he made me call you."

Vince tried to aim at Nikolai. "Stay calm, Linka. He won't hurt you."

Nikolai, by the wobbling on his feet was not only stupid but drunk too. He waved a Glock at Vince and fired.

Vince ducked as bits of wood sprayed over the stairs.

Nikolai held Angelika as a human shield. "I will not only hurt her, but I'll kill her if it will hurt you, you son of a bitch."

Vince attempted to take aim at Nikolai but the bastard kept bobbing behind Linka.

"My wife." Nikolai glared from behind Linka. "I've been looking for you in the U.S. and you've been here spending time with my wife."

Vince looked up through the rails and grinned.

I'll piss him off and make him screw up so I can take him out once and for all.

"I have enjoyed the pleasure of your wife's company."

Nikolai fired another shot but missed again. "She would never betray me."

"Wouldn't she? Women have needs too." Vince continued looking for a clear shot. "All those workouts have paid off. She's got a tight little body. Now she wants more. Who can blame her?"

Another shot from Nikolai missed. "You lie."

"Why should she wait around for you when I'm right here, ready to satisfy her every need?"

Nikolai tightened his grip on Linka.

Her face was turning red.

"Let the old woman go, Nikolai. Don't be a coward. Let's settle this like men."

The door downstairs burst open and Sasha and his men came storming up the stairs, guns drawn. "Vika!"

Nikolai threw Linka onto the rail and Vince caught her before she tumbled onto the stairs below.

Sasha and his men chased Nikolai through Linka's apartment. Sasha returned a few moments later to find Vince setting Linka on the couch. "He got away across the roof. He had a driver waiting. We heard the car driving away. He's in the city now. Our men will catch him."

Linka was calm. She put a hand on Vince's. "Vika, I've seen you with Sveta. It isn't Nikolai's wife you're after, it is him isn't it? He is your personal business."

A wave of regret for involving Linka rushed over Vince. "I'm so sorry, Linka. I never meant to put you in danger. I'll move out today."

She patted his hand. "Don't be silly, Vika. You'll stay right here." She looked over at Sasha. "Sasha, call my son. I don't want that man or his men anywhere near my home again."

"Of course." Sasha dialed quickly.

Vince listened to the call and put it all together. The Mikhailovich was Linka's son. Nikolai had just committed the deadliest of all sins. He'd manhandled the boss' mother.

I'm no less guilty. I led Nikolai here.

Sasha hung up and turned to Linka. "We'll stay with you and my men will keep watch outside. Vika, may I speak to you in the hall?"

Dread curled through Vince's gut.

This could be bad.

Sasha closed the door behind them. "He found out about you spending time with his wife?"

"Sasha, I knew he'd come for me but I never thought he'd involve civilians."

"Well, my friend, he involved the wrong civilian." Sasha nodded toward Linka's door.

"I had no idea she was the Mikhailovich's mother."

Sasha bit his bottom lip and nodded. "Apparently neither did Federov. He's on the dead list now. Our orders are to kill him on sight."

~~~

Vince watched as the bartender at Sasha''s nightclub counted the cash, placed it in a deposit bag, and gave the bag to Sasha. "You do a good business here."

"This operation is small time. I have girls and drugs in the back and clean the money in the front."

As if on cue, one of the girls came in from the back and handed Sasha a bag twice the size of the first one.

"I have a plan for my future. The real money is in uranium and international banking fraud. I figure I distinguish myself and they'll bring me into one of their banks."

Vince smiled and shook his head. *A smart criminal with a plan.* He had to admit Sasha was a likeable guy and hadn't done anything worse than he himself had done in the line of duty.

A soldier is a soldier. Right and wrong are subjective.

"Remember that woman I told you my friend flew into Afghanistan?" Sasha made an hourglass figure in the air with his hands.

"How could I forget? You got another story?"

Please be good news.

"Yeah. You know how she got into business?" He didn't wait for Vince to answer. "She got into business by killing her lovers and taking their money."

And she's being talked about in Russian bars. That's our Sarah. Good girl.

Feeling playful, Vince yanked Sasha's chain. "Come on. You expect me to believe that?"

"Yes, it is true!"

Yeah, Sarah is good like that. Her truth is stranger than fiction.

"She hooked up with this rich guy, Hassan. I know a guy who went to a party on his yacht. Real nice yacht. Everything was first class."

I remember.

"Sasha? The story?"

"She killed Hassan and made off with all his money. Then she hooked up with this guy in the Ivanov Organization. He ran guns and an air transport business. She killed him and took over his transportation routes."

In actuality, I was the one who made the kill shot.

" That's way too much to believe. Are you telling me she stole one guy's money and another guy's planes? What else have you got, Sasha?"

"No, she took the money from the first guy and started a shipping business after putting the second guy down so he couldn't compete with her business. Now she runs all the roads from Afghanistan to the United States."

That's a lot of road. Way to go, girl.

"What did you say her name was again?"

"Why? You want to call her up? People call her Scuro to her face but she's known as The Black Widow."

The Black Widow. That's great. She's a legend now. She's not just an agent anymore. She's a weapon.

Vince grinned into his beer. "I like a woman who keeps herself busy."

"Of course. I do too. But she's beautiful. Every man she meets wants to be with her and she kills them all!"

Not all of us.

"But what a way to go."

Sasha slapped Vince on the back. "You got that right, my friend!"

Sixteen

Moscow

Vince sipped his tonic water as Sasha waved the tassled dancer away and answered his ringing phone. Vince tried to listen but the music at Sasha's club was much too loud.

Sasha nodded several times before hanging up and slipping his phone back in his breast pocket. "There is a shodka, a gangsters' meeting, in the country this weekend. They want to know about your relationship with Federov. You can stay at my dacha."

Vince eyed Sasha. "What are the odds of me getting out alive?"

"With me? Pretty good. You aren't in trouble, Vika. If you were, I wouldn't suggest we make a party of it and bring some girls. Do you have one or should I get you a couple?"

"Are you sure it's safe?"

"My friend! You saved the boss' mother. You're a fucking hero!"

"How exactly is that anyway? Why is she in a little apartment instead of in a secure mansion?"

"Misha only had a daughter by his wife before she died. He had his son by Linka. He's a bastard but a son is a son." Misha tried to give Linka a mansion and gifts but the woman is shrewd. She asked for property instead. She keeps a low profile but she owns a good chunk of Moscow.

~~~

Linka poured the tea. "You'll go to the dacha this weekend?"

"Yes. Apparently my attendance is required. Whatever happens, I am very sorry you were involved."

The old woman smiled and patted his hand. "Ah, Vika. It is not what you think. My son would no sooner harm you than he would me." She winked. "I've made sure of that." She took a tentative sip of her tea. "You must go to Sasha's dacha and enjoy yourself. Bring Sveta. It will be nice for her."

Peredelkino, Russia

Vince pulled his Jeep up behind Sasha's BMW in the long driveway lined with trees. The house was a large two-story Victorian mansion that appeared big enough to comfortably house a family of ten.

Sasha stepped out of his car and smiled at Vince. "Welcome to our little country place. Sveta, Valentina will show you around. Valentina, my dear wife, make her comfortable, prepare the shashlik, and we will be back to tend the fire and cook the meat."

"Vika, we'll take my car."

Vince kissed Sveta on the cheek and hopped in the passenger seat of Sasha's BMW. He knew full well this might be the most demanding interrogation he would ever go through. He recalled all the events in his favor, all the things he'd done for the organization as well as having Linka as a personal friend. These things had to count for something in the grand scheme.

Sasha drove to another mansion several miles away. They pulled up to a covered carport and left the keys in the car. As they walked up the front steps, a young man scurried to the car and drove away.

Vince glanced at Sasha. "Valet?"

Sasha shrugged. "Of course."

They were met just inside the door by armed guards who scanned and searched them for weapons.

Sasha spread his arms wide. "Welcome to the Thieves' World. This is a kingpin gathering. It is our government. We discuss and make decisions here. There will be a coronation this weekend and we'll also discuss this issue you have with Federov. You will give evidence. I should not need to stress the importance of complete transparency. You don't want to make these guys angry."

"I can see that."

An armed guard escorted Vince into a large formal parlor. Eight men seated in a semi-circle inside wore fine suits and looked more like a board of directors than a bunch of gangsters.

Misha nodded when his gaze met Vince's and spoke first. "Vika, welcome." He motioned to a solitary chair that faced the other men. "Please sit."

"Thank you." Vince carefully sat in the chair, head up, shoulders straight, and looked each man in the eye.

Mikhail spoke. "You know why you are here. You are not in danger but we must know more about you and the business that brings you here."

"I am an American. I was in Italy recently and kidnapped at the airport. I was brought to Saudi Arabia, held prisoner and beaten for days. My host was about to have me put down when I managed to escape. When he left Saudi Arabia, he came to Moscow. You know him. His name is Nikolai Federov."

"Federov kidnapped you?"

"Yes. I came here to kill him."

"Why haven't you?"

"Because I couldn't risk Linka's life. I want him dead but I'll do it without hurting women and children in the process."

"What will you do when he is dead? Will you return to the United States?"

Vince knew he'd be taking a calculated risk by being completely honest, but he felt confident he could protect Sveta and trusted these men would respect a sense of honor.

"I'd like to stay here and marry the woman carrying my child."

The kingpins showed no emotion except for Mikhail who held back the hint of a smile and nodded at Vince. "You may go while we discuss this. Go to Sasha's dacha and wait.

~~~

Sasha turned the skewered meat and vegetables they called shashlik and looked around at his large backyard covered in snow. The grill sizzled with the juices of meat and vegetables. "You should see this place in the summer. Beautiful."

Vince warmed his hands by the barbeque grill. "I'll bet it makes for great weekends. Sasha, you know why I came here and you know why I stay now. Isn't it time you tell me what the real story is with Federov?"

"Federov is a boss, not a kingpin, and a disliked boss at that. His business has suffered lately and the Ivanov is not happy with him. He's a freeze-off."

"What's that?" Vince grabbed a piece of onion that had come loose from a skewer and popped the warm vegetable in his mouth.

"He thought he could crown himself kingpin, and that, my friend, is not how things are done. We'll suffer no discipline if we make him go away. It may even be a point of cooperation for us and the Ivanov."

"So he tried to buck rank?" Vince rubbed his hands over the fire.

"That is exactly what he did. A kingpin is a respected, experienced career criminal whose opinion cannot be ignored in the underworld. He is crowned in a secret ceremony that cannot be conducted without full compliance with the kingpin law. During the last shodka, Federov jumped up on the table and declared himself a kingpin as everyone was leaving. They paid him no mind and didn't give it a second thought because he left the country immediately afterward. They all thought he left out of shame and went off, perhaps, to make some extra money to buy back some respect from the other kingpins."

Vince caught a healthy whiff of the cooking meat and his stomach growled. "So what happened?"

"He tried to bump some bosses' territories but they fought back. He came back having lost money and the Ivanov's transporter in the process. That incident with Linka was his last desperate act."

"There is no honor in any of that."

"That is the problem. He doesn't follow our code of honor. He shows no respect for his superiors and assumes he can just take rank that isn't his."

Sasha's phone rang. "Excuse me." He pulled it from his coat pocket and answered. "This is Sasha." He looked up at Vince. "Yes, I understand." He nodded. "Thank you." He closed the phone and slipped it back into his pocket without looking at Vince.

Dread colder than the winter night crept up Vince's spine.

Why isn't he saying anything?

Sveta walked out onto the patio and gave them each a glass of vodka. "I thought you might be cold."

"Just in time!" Sasha grinned at Vince. "Congratulate your man. He is now a member of the family. Tomorrow he shall be baptized."

Sveta embraced Vince. "You have an even bigger family now. Congratulations, my dear."

Vince kissed her forehead. "It'll be your family too."

Sasha nearly choked on his vodka. "Oh, yes, I almost forgot! Mikhail has given you permission to marry his half-sister."

Vince's eyes opened wide as he looked down into Sveta's smiling face. "Why didn't you…?"

She shrugged. "I didn't think it was important."

Morocco

Sarah woke to the sound of a spoon on a saucer out on the balcony. She opened her eyes to the morning sunlight streaming in through the open French doors. A light breeze carried in the scent of salt and sea.

She stretched and sighed. She and Jay had made love all night and she was more than satisfied, and a little hungry.

Where does he get his stamina? Who cares? I love it.

She stood and slipped her robe on over her naked body, leaving the belt untied, and walked out to the balcony with a sleepy grin on her face.

Jay stood and wound his hands under her robe, pulling her naked body close to his. "Now that's how you should always dress for breakfast."

Enjoy A Sneak Peek Of Freedom's Price, Book 5

in the Task Force 125 Series

Chapter 1

Thick cloud cover inked out the sliver of a moon and added an eerie aura to deck of the aircraft carrier. Lieutenant Brian Allen popped a piece of gum in his mouth as he walked the staging area of the deck and surveyed the hustle around him. He listened as his SEAL team and their Royal Marine allies clicked magazines of ammunition into their weapons and completed function checks. He breathed in the salty Arabian Sea air as he embraced the pre-mission anticipation building inside him.

I love the smell of jet fuel in the morning.

The smell of jet fuel wafted across the deck as the Sikorsky helicopter's engine fired up. Their pilot began his preflight prep as the teams readied for combat. Bathed in the blue and green deck lights, the chopper had an otherworldly glow. She appeared as a dragon, a huge beast of war and destruction. Tonight's operation wasn't so much destruction as it was preventing it, though a small body count was expected for the Iraqis. The allies' mission was to land at the Al Basrah offshore oil terminal and take it before the retreating Iraqis blew it up. It was standard procedure for Saddam to order oil resources destroyed before the allies could capture them. If it was already rigged to blow, it would be Brian's team's job to disable the explosives and see that it didn't.

Brian patted the Sig Sauer handgun in his thigh holster and chambered a round in his M4A1 Carbine before looking at the faces of each of his four SEAL Fire Team members. "Ready to party?"

They shouted the affirmative "Hooah!"

Brian glanced over at his Royal Marine counterpart, a six-foot- three red-headed Scot who was built like a tank and could probably do as much damage. "Ready, Martin?"

Martin's green eyes sparkled as the blue and green deck lights reflected off the black greasepaint covering his face, giving him an almost serpentine quality. "Aye." Martin glanced at each of his four men in turn, apparently doing his own visual inspection. "Right, lads! Kit muster time is over. Lock and load!"

"Mount up, ladies! SEALs port, Marines starboard."

Their teams loaded into the open sided chopper, four men to each side, with their legs hanging out, ready to jump onto the deck of the oil terminal when the helicopter landed on it.

Brian and Martin climbed in last.

Whomp. The engine revved louder and the huge rotors began to spin slowly. *Whomp. Whomp.*

Brian's heart began to beat in time with the rotors as it always did before a mission. Something felt off tonight but he chalked it up to the enchiladas he'd had for dinner.

Whomp-whomp-whomp.

He breathed deep as the rotors spun the salty sea air around them and his blood raced. He lived for the adrenaline rush that missions brought with them. He was no different than the others.

Most of the men in special ops were adrenaline junkies and it suited them fine that way.

His breath quickened as the rotors worked up to their flying speed and a thrill raced through him as the bird lifted off the deck.

The men, packed in shoulder to shoulder inside, swayed with the chopper as it hovered over the deck for a moment, turned slowly, and then shot off at one-hundred-sixty miles per hour, flying low and fast, sandwiched between dark skies and deadly ocean.

They arrived at the oil platform in just minutes. The Sikorsky's nose pulled up for a quick stop where they'd planned for her to land and then take off again in seconds.

Brian tensed for the landing. "Ready, boys? Hop and pop."

"Hold up, LT!" The pilot turned to Brian. "We can't land. You're gonna have to jump it."

I could plan an operation for weeks, but nothing ever goes as planned.

These things happened, and Brian trusted the pilots he worked with. "Fast rope down?"

"Negative, sir. They've got c-wire about eighteen inches deep all over the deck. The rotor downwash could whip the rope and we'd get tangled. I'll hover as low as I can so you can jump from the skids."

Shit. Concertina wire, that spiral wire with razors attached to it every few inches. Great if you're behind it but you're guaranteed to bleed if you have to go through it.

Brian tensed his jaw and ground his teeth. He turned and grabbed Martin's huge shoulder before yelling into his ear so as to be heard over the whine of the engine and the thunder of the rotors. "C-wire on the deck. Gotta jump from the skids."

Martin nodded. "Right." Martin raised his voice so his men could hear him. "Oy, lads! Intel cocked up the recce. The LZ is laid with C-wire so it's time to go ninja!"

The men were all grunts and head nods. Going ninja was what they lived for.

Brian grinned. No matter what part of the world they came from, special forces troops all spoke the same language.

Martin hung on to the handle of the open side door and stepped onto the skid as the chopper lowered slowly over the woven mess of bloodthirsty wire. "Step lively, lads!"

Pride swelled in Brian for having the privilege of working with these men. Martin was a true leader by leading from the front and jumping in first. They'd all get tangled and chewed up in the wire and have some scars for it. As the first man in, Martin would take the brunt of the damage. With any luck they'd all live to tell the tale.

The pilot hovered the SeaHawk about seven feet above the platform.

The warm Arabian sea below the oil platform ebbed and flowed with its constant rhythm, filling Brian's lungs with the salty sear air he loved so much. Flashes of childhood summers on the beaches of Aquaba left his mind as quickly as they'd entered as shots rang out from below and Brian's training kicked in. "Deploy! Deploy! Hot LZ! Everybody out so we can get this chopper out of here!"

The Royal Marines and Brian's Navy SEALs jumped from the chopper like it was on fire.

Brian landed hard and crouched low in the concertina wire as the chopper cut away at top speed to avoid the barrage of bullets zinging toward it. The chopper's downdraft pushed the wire around the platform and into the men. Brian clenched his jaw and cursed at the sharp razors that dug into his calves but stayed low to avoid the enemy fire as he returned it.

We're surrounded. Somehow they knew we were coming.

His stomach tightened and heart beat loudly in his ears as he scanned the platform for the enemy shooters.

The Brits were tangled in the wire, but still moving slowly through it toward the outer perimeter of the platform where the Iraqis were lying low and raining down bullets on the two allied teams.

"Stay low!" Brian shouted as he returned fire. His and Martin's teams were completely surrounded, and the only way out was to shoot through hot lead.

"Bristol's down! Bulldog, watch your nine!" Martin was picking off as many of the Republican Guard as he could, but the allies were out manned and out gunned.

The rat-tat-tat of MP-5s slowed and Brian's heart rate shot up.

There should be more of our gunfire. Christ, I have men down!

The sharp, metal razors attached to the spiral bound wire grabbed at Brian's boots, tore at his trousers and sliced through the flesh on his calves as the Iraqis took shots at him and his team from all around the platform.

One of his men shouted gruffly from behind Brian. "Fuck! We're sitting ducks here, LT!"

Brian yelled over his shoulder. "Just stay low and lay it down, Wayne!" He turned to see where the rest of his SEALs were on the platform.

Davis is missing.

"Davis, status?" He shouted.

"Shit! Davis is down, LT!"

Brian's blood went cold. He looked over to where Davis should have been. Spencer crouched over him. "He's gone."

Fuck!

If they didn't want to be dead meatballs in this metallic spaghetti, they'd need to lay down a whole lot more fire.

Brian heard shots whizzing by and welcomed the music.

You never hear the one that kills you.

To his left, he saw one of his men crumple into the wire.

No, damnit!

Rage boiled inside him as Brian pinpointed the source of the shot and opened fire on three Republican Guards hunkered together. He knew they were dead when their guns stopped firing. He targeted the next source of gunfire and lay down a rain of bullets until his magazine was empty.

Reload. Silence.

Time to disarm the explosives the Republican Guards must certainly have set since they knew the allies were coming. "Martin, status?"

"Lost three. I've got one and me, LT. You?"

Brian turned to check on his men so they could regroup and move to their objective.

Four black clad SEAL bodies lay akimbo in the c-wire. "Jesus! Fuck!"

Brian gasped as he woke from the familiar dream. Sweat washed over his face and chest and the breeze from the air conditioner made it feel almost arctic in his luxury cabin on the yacht. He threw the sweaty bedding off himself and inhaled deeply, filling his lungs with the cool air that smelled of lavender air freshener rather than salty sea. He wiped the sweat from his face and ran his fingers through his wet hair.

Spy games with the CIA and living on a luxury yacht. I've come a long way in just a few years.

The new luxury yacht that served as the base of operations for American Swift was even better than the last but it couldn't sparkle enough to make the PTSD go away. He squeezed his eyes shut and ground his palms into his eyelids.

Good men gone and mourned by their families. Can I ever repay this debt I feel to them? Third time this week. Damnit. I need to see some action soon.

These were the ghosts driving Brian. Unless he was on a mission, unless he got that adrenaline fix, the flashbacks would continue to haunt him in his sleep. Post Traumatic Stress Disorder had a way of twisting every man's mind differently.

Sleep will be more and more difficult to come by unless I find an adrenaline fix soon. It's time I filed that transfer.

He walked to the bathroom, a private, marble encrusted shrine to the porcelain god. Stopping at the sink, he grasped the brushed nickel lever and pushed it back for some cold water. He splashed a few handfuls on his face and then dried off with the Ralph Lauren hand towel hanging nearby.

Too much luxury and too little reason for it.

He grabbed a file folder on his way out of the cabin and headed above deck to the office.

About The Author

Lisa Pietsch (pen name of Lisa Woodward) is the Publishing Director at Defiance Press and Publishing, an Air Force Veteran, former magazine publisher, multi-published author, mother of two giants, and wife to a Viking.

Lisa speaks French, Spanish, Norwegian, and Russian. She has been USAF Security Forces Leader, received specialized training as an FBI Hostage Negotiator, and worked with MI-5 on personal security details for both British and Jordanian Royals. These diverse experiences inspire her Task Force 125 series, which follows Sarah Stevens, a CIA Special Activities Division recruit, through gripping tales of espionage and paramilitary operations.

In 2020, Lisa's life took a romantic turn when she reconnected with the love of her life, the man who inspired her Task Force 125 series, launching her into her greatest adventure yet.

An avid gamer, Lisa enjoys both console and tabletop gaming, where she goes by "Geniekin" on Xbox and Roll20.

As Lisa Pietsch, she crafts thrilling paramilitary action/adventure/ romance novels, while as Lisa Woodward, she weaves enchanting epic romantic fantasy tales.

www.ingramcontent.com/pod-product-compliance
Lightning Source LLC
Chambersburg PA
CBHW051109030726
47504CB00006B/1857